Even if Justin remained friends with Marissa he'd be the third wheel, the odd man out, the one who would go home alone while they would have each other.

He wanted to be the one to enjoy Marissa's long legs wrapped around him, to see her shining smile, soothe her hurts and listen to her confidences.

He was right for her.

As he covertly studied her face, Justin thought of a dozen reasons why he should mind his own business and only one why he should not. By virtue of the lopsided number, logic overruled his wish to interfere, but suddenly it didn't matter if he had only one or a hundred justifiable motives to meddle. His single excuse overshadowed all others.

He wanted Marissa for himself.

Dear Reader

Welcome back to Hope City!

Have you ever been in a situation where you've taken things for granted and didn't truly realise or appreciate what you had until it was gone? In my fourth story of this series, Justin St James finds himself in the situation I've described. And once he makes that realisation he must find a way to win the heart of the woman he loves before it's too late.

Naturally, Marissa doesn't make life easy for him. After all, she's been under his nose for years and he hasn't noticed her, but she can't deny Justin's persistence as he struggles to convince her that she's HIS LONG-AWAITED BRIDE.

So find a comfy chair and enjoy Justin and Marissa's story!

Warmest wishes

Jessica Matthews

HIS
LONG-AWAITED
BRIDE

BY
JESSICA MATTHEWS

MILLS & BOON®
Pure reading pleasure

First published in Great Britain 2007
Large Print edition 2008
Harlequin Mills & Boon Limited,
Eton House, 18-24 Paradise Road,
Richmond, Surrey TW9 1SR

© Jessica Matthews 2007

ISBN: 978 0 263 19946 8

Set in Times Roman 16½ on 18½ pt.
17-0408-48714

Printed and bound in Great Britain
by Antony Rowe Ltd, Chippenham, Wiltshire

Jessica Matthews's interest in medicine began at a young age, and she nourished it with medical stories and hospital-based television programmes. After a stint as a teenage candy-striper, she pursued a career as a clinical laboratory scientist. When not writing or on duty she fills her day with countless family and school-related activities. Jessica lives in the central United States with her husband, daughter and son.

Recent titles by the same author:

THE GP'S VALENTINE PROPOSAL
THE BABY RESCUE
SAVING DR TREMAINE

To Maggie, Sue, and Pam.

You gave me more support than you'll
ever know during a trying time in my life.

You're three in a million!

CHAPTER ONE

SHE had to hide the evidence.

Marissa Benson stared at the bouquets lining the counter of Hope City Hospital's intensive care unit, hardly able to believe that her perfectly normal morning had become the opposite in the space of a few minutes. While the unexpected was only to be expected in any hospital, she had never dreamed that one minute she would be snowed under with doctors orders and the next she would be standing up to her earlobes in flower petals.

"You must have had some date last night," fellow nurse Kristi Thomas teased with a glint in her eyes. "I've never gone out with anyone who sent flowers the next day."

"We had a nice time," Marissa said primly. Although she and Kristi were both single and often compared notes on their dating experiences, the details of her evening were still too special to share, even with someone as close as Kristi.

Kristi leaned over to sniff a carnation. "Come on, lady. 'Fess up. Where did you *find* this guy?"

Marissa grinned. "At the health spa. He took the treadmill next to mine."

Kristi grimaced. "Ouch. Exercise. Still…" Her tone grew thoughtful. "If working out yields results like this, I may have to reconsider. Does he have a footloose brother or cousin hanging around?"

"No to the brother. Don't know about the cousin."

"Well, find out. That is, if you ever get to the talking stage."

"We talk a lot," Marissa protested at Kristi's teasing wink. "In fact, last night we talked all though dinner and for hours after the community theatre performance."

Kristi smirked. "Yeah, right. If you say so."

"I do." The words sent a fresh surge of heat to her face as she remembered…. "Look," she said, certain that she was grinning like a loon, "it isn't that I don't want to tell you, but—"

Kristi stepped up and hugged her. "I know. Some

things are so good that you have to hold them inside and savor them for a while. I understand."

"Thanks."

"Just promise me this. When you're ready to tell all, I'm first to hear the scoop."

Marissa laughed. "I promise."

"Now that you've hooked yourself a winner, throw any others you find my way."

"I will."

Kristi's smile faded as she touched a rose petal. "It's too bad these didn't arrive before you went off duty. Now you have to stash them out of sight until you leave. And pronto."

It didn't seem fair that such a thoughtful and flattering gesture would also create a monumental headache. Marissa sighed. "My thoughts exactly. If I wait until the end of my shift, Lorraine will go ballistic."

Lorraine Hawthorne was the sixty-two-year-old director of nursing who firmly believed that flowers didn't belong in the ICU. If a patient was well enough to enjoy them, she claimed, then they didn't belong in the unit. And while that might be true to a certain extent, a cheerful spray of color on the nurses' station counter gave a spiritual boost to everyone who passed by.

Unfortunately, a small, cheerful spray of color was one thing. *Seven* bouquets fell into the ostentatious category.

"Any ideas?" Marissa asked.

"Other than an empty patient room, not one."

"That would work, I suppose," she said as she tried the suggestion on for size. "I could close the privacy curtains and no one would see."

"If the boss walks in, she'll wonder why the drapes are pulled," Kristi warned. "And if we get another patient…"

Marissa didn't need Kristi to finish her sentence. A new admission would only mean she'd have to move her flowers again. The place she chose had to be secure enough to avoid discovery for the entire day.

"What are you going to do?" Kristi asked, her expression a mixture of concern, curiosity and envy.

Marissa glanced at her floral line-up. While she was thrilled by Travis's grandstand gesture, she wondered what he'd been thinking. Her work environment wasn't flower-friendly, and even if it had been, how had he expected her to take them home? Her compact two-door car didn't have the cargo space of an SUV or minivan.

The flowers simply had to go.

"First things first," she decided. "I'll move them out of sight before anyone notices."

"Anyone as in *everyone*, or anyone as in a certain person who can melt her subordinates with one glare?" drawled a familiar voice from behind a rhododendron, seconds before a man pushed aside the plant to reveal himself.

It took Marissa the length of a heartbeat to identify the visitor, although she almost wished that someone other than Justin St. James had arrived. While he was a good friend from her college days, as well as one of the two internal medicine specialists on staff, he also had an uncanny tendency to stick his nose into her business.

His *perfect*, aristocratic nose. Then again, everything about him was perfect as far as Marissa could tell. Tall, dark and handsome might be a clichéd description, but it fit Justin like a professionally tailored suit. Strong shoulders, a lean physique, chocolaty brown eyes to match his hair and a smile that melted women's knees—her own included—made Dr. St. James dream material.

And best of all, his physical appearance notwithstanding, his personality only added to his allure. He had what Marissa called the three *P*s—he was polite, patient and persistent, all of which ranked him number one in the bedside-manner department. In fact, if Marissa had to point out a flaw, the only thing she could say was that he worked too hard. And that he looked at her as if she were his younger sister.

More was the pity. Her only consolation was that she'd known for years that she wasn't his type—sophisticated, blond and beauty-queen gorgeous—and had resigned herself to that fact long ago. It was futile to wish for more, even though she indulged herself on occasion. After all, what was the harm in fantasizing about a tall, dark and handsome fellow with a grin—and gorgeous buns—to die for?

Actually, she knew the harm, which was why she only let her imagination run wild on rare occasions. It was less disappointing that way.

"Anyone as in *everyone*," Marissa repeated seriously, "although you're an exception."

Justin grinned. "I am? I'm flattered."

"Don't be," she said with a smile. "It's only because you can be bribed with a home-cooked meal. What'll it be this time? American, Chinese, Italian or Mexican?"

He stepped into the nurses' station and, like always, his presence filled the area much like his broad shoulders filled out his blue dress shirt. "Surprise me, but cherry cheesecake is part of the deal."

"Fine. In the meantime, make yourself useful." She thrust the vase of roses into his startled grasp, then the rhododendron.

"Hey," he protested, "since when did the *D* in 'MD' stand for Delivery?"

"Since I need an extra pair of hands and yours are the only ones available. Need I remind you that if Lorraine sees these and reads me the Riot Act, you can tell your tastebuds to think hospital cafeteria tuna surprise instead of jalapeño and melted cheese?"

"All right, all right," he grumbled good-naturedly. "But make it fast. I have places to go and people to see."

"Don't we all?" she answered dryly. "Now, to find a perfect hiding place…" She glanced down the hallway in search of inspiration.

"How about the storeroom?" Kristi offered. "OB borrowed a couple of our wheelchairs so we have some extra space until they bring them back."

"Good idea." Marissa left the salmon-colored Gerbera daisy in its yellow ceramic pot on the counter next to the large spray of carnations and baby's breath and followed Kristi down the corridor. Justin fell into step beside her.

"What's the occasion?" he asked, his curiosity palpable. "I know it isn't your birthday."

Before Marissa could frame her answer, Kristi beat her to the punch.

"They're from her date last night," Kristi supplied in a dreamy voice as she unlocked the supply-room door and opened it with a flourish. "Lucky girl. Isn't it romantic?"

Justin's jaw dropped in obvious surprise. "From your date?" he said.

Marissa nudged past him to place her armload

on an empty shelf. "Yes," she answered simply as she avoided his gaze, well aware that more questions would be coming—questions that she didn't want to answer in such a public place. "Let me have those," she said instead, as she took the arrangements out of his hands and placed them on an empty metal cart.

An instant later, she shooed her two helpers from the room and closed the door with a decided click. "Thanks for your help in buying me some time," she told them.

"What're friends for?" Kristi winked. Before anything else could be said, a call light blinked down the hall. "That's for me," she said cheerfully, leaving Marissa and Justin alone. As Marissa had suspected, it didn't take long for the inquisition to begin.

"You got all this after going out with what's his name?"

The disbelief in his voice, as if it was completely inconceivable that a man would go to such lengths for her, instantly added starch to Marissa's spine. It was bad enough that Justin had never noticed her, not even during those carefree college days when she had been his study buddy and he had dated what had seemed like every woman in her entire dormitory. The idea that he still couldn't see her as a woman who might attract a man and enamor him to reckless generosity was enough to raise her hackles.

"Is it completely beyond the realm of possibility for me to receive flowers?" she demanded.

"No, but considering today isn't your birthday and you're not celebrating an anniversary, this seems a little..." He stopped short, as if he'd finally noticed her clenched jaw and narrowed eyes, and had decided it was time to tread softly.

"Bizarre? Overboard?" She faced him squarely, daring him to agree with her.

He didn't. "What *is* the occasion?"

"Does a man need an *occasion* to send flowers?" she countered. "Can't he give a bouquet for no other reason than just because he wants to? Or because he knows it would make a girl feel special?"

"If it was one bouquet, I'd agree with you, but he's cleaned out the florist's shop. He either wants something or buddy boy's a showboat," he finished, the disgust in his voice as obvious as the look on his face.

"You're jealous."

"Jealous? Of what?"

His clueless attitude caused her teeth to grind together painfully. Those three little words only drove home how smart she'd been way back when to accept their platonic relationship and move on to greener pastures.

"That he thought of doing something kind and considerate and you didn't."

He rolled his eyes. "Oh, ple-e-ease."

"It's true. When was the last time you sent anyone flowers for no other reason than 'just because'?"

He opened his mouth to speak, then closed it.

"Aha!" she crowed. "I knew it. You never have."

"Hey, if Trevor wants to—"

"You're definitely suffering from a senior moment," she interrupted grimly. "I'll remind you that his name is Travis. Travis Pendleton."

"Whatever." He waved his mistake aside with one hand.

She strode toward the nurses' station, intent

on the last of the large floral arrangements still standing on the counter. Although she'd hoped to leave him behind, he caught up to her in spite of her two-step head start.

"This was, what, your second date?" he asked.

"Third," she corrected.

"Ah, yes. Number three. A regular milestone in a relationship."

She grabbed the vase before she faced him with narrowed eyes. "What's that supposed to mean? Just because you don't date and if you do, it's never more than twice..."

He held up his hands. "Hey, if Trevor wants to spend a fortune on flowers, I'm sure that Frannie's Florals will be delighted to get the business. But it might be a good idea if you told him to send flowers to your home address instead of here. I may not be able to bail you out the next time."

"Bail me out?" she sputtered.

"Not to mention it makes the place look like a damn funeral parlor," he continued mercilessly. "We're here to take care of patients, not to smell the roses."

"I didn't ask for any of this," Marissa said defensively. Angry and hurt, not to mention bewildered by his attack, she squared her shoulders and adopted her most professional tone. "But you're right, *Doctor*. We're here for patients, so if you'll excuse me, I have work to do."

She regally sailed past the centrally located nurses' station to room six, leaving Justin behind. With luck, by the time she left Lonnie Newland's bedside, Justin would have reviewed his charts and left her unit—and her—in peace.

Fat chance. Lonnie was also Justin's patient, which meant she'd have to discuss the man's care with him shortly, but at least Justin would have to focus on something other than her personal life. And she could concentrate on issues other than how she'd like to knock a bedpan—preferably a used one—against his hard head.

Before she crossed the threshold of the cubicle, she drew a deep breath, forced a smile to her lips and greeted Lonnie's wife, the thirtyish woman who was gently washing her husband's stubbled face.

"Hi, Abby," Marissa greeted her. "I brought a little something to brighten up the place."

Abby's soft smile didn't quite reach her eyes, which wasn't surprising under the circumstances. The dark circles and tired droop of her shoulders were easily explained by her pregnancy and the stress of having had a comatose husband for the past three months. Lonnie had been riding his motorcycle on his way home from Kansas City when a car had hit him. In spite of wearing his protective helmet, he'd been left with massive head injuries and had only recently been transferred back home to Hope Memorial after the neurology unit had done all it could. After a brief stint in the long-term care annex, where he'd developed a kidney infection, Lonnie had been transferred back into ICU.

"Thanks, Marissa. We're going to enjoy them a lot, aren't we, Lonnie?"

It was obvious that Abby had taken the neurosurgeon's advice to heart. She talked to her husband as if he were awake and able to respond, determined to provide any and all possible stimulation she could to draw him out of his unconscious state.

She leaned close to her husband's ear as she touched his pale arm. "You should see what Marissa brought us. The carnations are just lovely. They remind me of the bouquet you sent me when we first heard the news about the baby. They're pink and yellow and blue with lots of baby's breath and greenery. We're going to put them on the tray table in front of you so you can smell them."

Marissa placed the vase where Abby had requested, wishing—no, *hoping*—that the smell of the fragrant blooms, coupled with his wife's voice, would be enough to yank the thirty-five-year-old businessman back to the land of the living. Logically, however, and based upon her experience, the situation didn't bode well for a happy ending. On the other hand, she'd been an ICU nurse for too long to discount the possibility of a miracle or the power of hope.

"Did you get any rest last night?" she asked Abby while she monitored Lonnie's vital signs and checked everything from his IV sites to drainage tubes.

"Some," Abby admitted. "It's just hard to be at

home by myself. Even when my sister or parents come to visit, the house seems so empty…." Her voice died as she shrugged a slim shoulder.

Although Marissa couldn't claim to know precisely what Abby was feeling, she did know how empty and lifeless her own house seemed at times. More often than not, she sensed it after one of Justin's lengthy visits when they played Scrabble or indulged in one of their movie marathons until the wee hours. Strange how she didn't experience that same phenomenon with anyone else….

"But I'm not totally alone," Abby said with a smile as she rubbed her swollen abdomen. "The baby's been a big help already."

"I'm glad." It was anyone's guess what condition Lonnie would be in when he regained consciousness. He could need months and years of therapy before he could go home. *If* he could ever go home at all. Abby's son or daughter would give her something to hold on to no matter what the future held.

Abby motioned to the small spiral notebook that held Marissa's findings. "How's he doing?"

In lieu of good news, she opted for the stock answer. "He's holding his own."

Abby's smile wavered. "That's better than the alternative, isn't it?"

"Absolutely." Marissa supposed it was a case of seeing a glass as either half-empty or half-full. A report of "No change" might not be a strong ray of hope, but it was better than "His condition is deteriorating."

Before Abby could ask more questions, Marissa posed one of her own. "What are your plans today?"

"I thought I'd read to him this morning," Abby said. "I brought *Oliver Twist*."

"'Please, sir, may I have some more?'" Marissa quoted.

"Then you've read the story?"

"Read the story, seen the movie. Although, to be honest, I liked the movie version better." Marissa grinned. "And that's the only line I remember, but don't tell anyone."

Abby giggled. "It'll be our secret." She stroked her husband's face. "Isn't that right, dear?"

Suspecting that Abby would read until she was hoarse, Marissa cautioned her not to overdo it.

"Oh, I won't. You see, I have a doctor's appointment this afternoon. Then it'll be nap time—doctor's orders," she added ruefully. "So I won't come back until after dinner. You'll call me if…"

"There's any change," Marissa promised, as she always did. "Your number is posted in the nurses' station. By the way, aren't your childbirth classes starting soon?"

Abby rubbed her tummy once again. "This week."

"Do you have a labor coach?"

"With my parents and sister living so far away, Lonnie's brother, Eric, has offered to stand in."

"I'm glad you have someone, but don't hesitate to call if you need me." Marissa had given Abby both her home phone and cellphone numbers several weeks previously as an emergency contact. It seemed the least she could do for the new mother in such a sad situation.

"Believe me, I won't." Abby patted her stomach. "I'm not about to take any chances with Junior."

Marissa nodded, well aware that this baby was surrounded with love and care even without Abby's firm assurance. And while she might not be able to do as much for Abby as she would like, the one thing she *could* do was to give Abby's husband the best possible nursing that she could provide. With any luck, he might be alert when his son or daughter arrived in a few short weeks.

She cast a final glance at the array of monitors above her patient's head. Satisfied by the readings, she deftly adjusted the blanket over Lonnie's feet. "I'll leave you two alone for now," she said with a smile. "If you need anything, I'm only a few steps away."

Her calm deserted her the moment she left the room. Determined to ignore Justin as much as possible, or at least to treat him with cool indifference, she crossed into the nurses' station, braced for a fight.

To her surprise, Justin was noticeably absent.

He hadn't seen his patient, so he couldn't have gone far.

"Where's Dr. St. James?" she asked Kristi, hating to ask in case he was within earshot.

"Dr. Tremaine paged him for the ER. He left about ten minutes ago, and said he'd be back as soon as he could. Do you need him?"

Need Justin St. James? Hardly, she inwardly scoffed. "Not at the moment. I just didn't want him to get away without rewriting a medication order." Then, because she wanted to push the man from her mind, she changed the subject. "I noticed we're low on syringes and blood-gas kits. Before I check through the drawers, can you think of anything else to add to my order?"

"Not right now."

Marissa nodded. As she compared her checklist to the labeled cupboards and drawers in the small medication room adjoining the nurses' station, she wished that her life was as neatly arranged.

Maybe that was all it took—a checklist. Let's see, she thought as she started a mental tally. She had a house that suited her perfectly, even if it was on the small side. A Cairn terrier that served as companion and confidant. Wonderful neighbors, especially Lucy Mullins next door. She also had great friends and lived in a community that boasted enough shopping opportunities and free-time activities to keep her happy. What more could a girl want?

A husband. A couple of kids. A family.

Okay, so those things were missing. And, yes, she admitted, those were major items for a woman who had been raised by her grandmother, thanks to her mother's parade of husbands who hadn't been interested in having a stepdaughter underfoot. The fact that she wanted a family at all was a testament to her grandmother's moral fiber and value system. If she'd actually lived with her mother during the turbulence of all her marriages, she might have felt differently, but her grandmother had been her anchor and her role model.

The one thing she *had* learned from her mother was not to be taken in by a charming smile and a handsome face. While she considered herself "cautious" when it came to the opposite sex, some might call her "picky." Admittedly, she was, although she'd dreamed of having her family—or at least a husband—by the time she hit thirty. She had a year to go before she missed her self-imposed deadline.

Of all the men she'd ever dated, Travis Pendleton had the most potential of being The One. And if their relationship continued to move along as well and as fast as it had so far, she just might be on the way to realizing her dream with time to spare.

Idly, she wondered how Justin would react to news of her getting married. He'd be shocked, to be sure, and would try to change her mind, but if this was the right thing for her to do, then nothing would stand in her way.

But, oh, how she'd love to see the look on his face when she told him....

Justin lingered at the far end of the nurses' station, out of Marissa's sight as she sat in front of a computer terminal. She seemed in a good mood, which was a relief considering the way they'd parted thirty minutes ago. Even if she hadn't been, he'd always been able to wiggle his way back into her good graces. He felt certain he could do so again.

Do you really think so? his little voice asked.

It might not be as easy this time, he admitted. Discrediting the man who'd provided more bouquets than most women saw in a lifetime hadn't been the smartest thing he'd ever done. He should have known that she'd feel compelled to defend the man. The problem was, he didn't quite understand why his temper had suddenly flared at the mention of Pendleton and his dramatic gesture.

You're jealous.

Hardly, he scoffed at Marissa's words echoing in his mind. He simply didn't want her to be taken in by a man who was all flash and no substance. If he could save an old friend from making the same mistakes that he had, he would. His motives were as simple as that.

And, yes, Marissa had a good, level head on those pretty shoulders. She could size up a fellow quite well, but none of them had ever gone to such drastic lengths to impress her. What woman wouldn't be affected by the romance of this grandstand gesture? It was his *duty* to make sure that an undeserving lout didn't hang stars in her eyes now, only to blast them to earth later.

Even now, he swore he could smell flowers, although it was probably all in his imagination. That, or the fact that the scent of those damn roses he'd carried had rubbed off on his clothes.

Just as he was about to make his presence known and tell her about his new ICU admission, the phone rang to give him a brief reprieve.

He watched and listened as she spoke with the usual joyful lilt in her voice. From past experience, he knew that one didn't have to see her to hear her perpetual smile. It was why he always made a point to talk to her either in person or on the phone at the end of the day. Just the sound of her voice lifted his spirits, no matter what his mood.

Her long, light-brown hair was tied back in a ponytail instead of a braid, which meant that she'd probably overslept that morning. It made her appear too young to be the shift charge nurse, but those who were foolish enough to think that a youthful appearance and medical experience couldn't coexist soon learned otherwise.

She tucked an ink pen behind her ear, drawing his attention to her fine features. Even from his position, he could see the gentle curve of her mouth as she reached out to caress one of the daisy petals with long, slender fingers. He knew just how gentle her touch was—he'd seen her work her magic with her patients and had enjoyed more than one of her back rubs when he'd been dead tired.

To him, though, her hazel eyes, framed with dark lashes, were her best feature. Gazing into them was like watching the different moods of the Atlantic, but whether they sparkled with animation or reflected her genuine care and compassion, they didn't reveal a lot of what was going on inside her pretty head. For all her friendliness and the years they'd known each other, she was still, in effect, a private person.

Sometimes, like now, he wondered why she hadn't found the right man to spend her life with, but considering her mother was on husband number four, he understood why she hadn't rushed into the state of matrimony.

Her mother's failed marriages aside, he chose to take a small amount of credit for Marissa's caution. After his own marital fiasco, he'd vowed that none of his friends would be taken in by a pretty face or, in Marissa's case, a handsome one. No, siree. It wouldn't happen on his watch.

Perhaps he wouldn't feel this strongly if someone had warned him about his ex-wife,

Chandra. Her gorgeous face and model's body had hidden a calculating mind and a hard, greedy heart. Within six months of their wedding, she'd maxed their credit cards to the limit "because you'll be able to afford it, darling. And I have an image to uphold," she'd cooed.

Some image. He grimaced at the memory. Sleeping with the bank loan officer who'd been helping them obtain the funds for their first home had certainly not been upholding *his* ideal image of a trustworthy physician or a happy marriage. Neither was having an affair with their accountant, her dentist or their veterinarian. By then, her escapades had killed any feelings he'd had for her.

Had he loved her? He'd thought so at the time, but now he couldn't say. True love couldn't be killed so quickly, could it? After all, he missed Maisie, Chandra's French poodle, more than he missed her.

In any event, she'd eventually walked out because she'd been tired of trying to make their marriage work when she hadn't loved him. Privately, he doubted if she ever had. She may have loved him for his profession, his future income and his status, but not for *him*. If he hadn't been so blinded by lust, he might have seen the same character flaw that his closest friends in med school had seen. But he hadn't, and they hadn't uttered a single word. "We hoped we were wrong," they'd said in their defense.

Unfortunately, they hadn't been. Now, having been burned by his experience, he'd never sleep at night knowing that he could have saved a friend from misery and hadn't.

Be that as it may, their personal issues and discussion would have to wait. The soon-to-arrive patient would take precedence.

He approached Marissa as she severed the phone connection. "I'm back," he announced.

The smile on her face faded. "How nice."

Her polite tone grated on his nerves but he deserved a chilly reception. Before he could frame an apology, she pointed to the monitor of a second computer. "My notes on Mr. Newland are charted for your review. The pharmacy has already called about renewing his medication orders, so if you can take care of that first—"

"They'll have to wait. I'm admitting a new patient to the unit, a seventy-year-old female with possible meningitis or encephalitis. I'll want a spinal tap." The elevator bell dinged an interruption, and he added, "That's probably her now."

She rose and darted around the counter, her cool demeanor changing to her usual professionalism. "I'll put her in two."

"Marissa, wait."

She stopped in her tracks. "Why? Your patient is here."

As if he needed a reminder. "I know." He paused. "You need to know something first."

Impatience flitted across her face. "What?"

"It's Lucy."

"Lucy who?"

"Lucy Mullins."

It took a second for the name to register. Her eyes widened and her jaw dropped. "*My* Lucy?"

He nodded, intently watching her response.

Lucy Mullins might be Marissa's seventy-year-old neighbor, but she was far more than that. Neither woman had any family to speak of, and he knew that Lucy offered friendship, homemade cookies and motherly advice whenever any of the above were needed.

The worry in Marissa's eyes turned to determination. "As soon as I've gotten her settled into room two and am ready for the spinal tap, I'll let you know."

She headed in that direction, but Justin's hand on her arm held her in place. "What now?" she asked impatiently.

"Ask Kristi to take over for you."

She stared at him, incredulous. "Why? Lucy is my patient."

He shook his head, aware that she wouldn't like what he would say next any better than she'd liked his comments about Pendleton. "Not today she isn't."

CHAPTER TWO

JUSTIN braced himself for her inevitable outburst and hoped he could make her see reason.

"What do you mean, she isn't my patient?" Marissa demanded, her eyes flashing fire.

"Just that."

"Of course she's my patient," she snapped. "Not only do I have two patients to Kristi's three, but I'm in charge of nursing assignments."

Her emphasis on *I* didn't escape him, but he knew it would be better for all concerned if Marissa stepped aside. "You're too close to the situation," he pointed out. "You won't be objective."

"I won't be objective?" she sputtered.

"This isn't any different than a physician treating a family member," he countered. "So don't get all up in arms about it. I just think—"

Marissa leaned close enough that he could feel

her breath whisper across his chin. "Don't. Don't think at all, because you can't stop me from making a nursing decision. You *won't* stop me from looking after Lucy. I'm the senior nurse on this unit and I—not you—make the patient assignments."

He'd hoped this would be easy, although he knew before he left the ER that it wouldn't. "I can go over your head. And if I do, you know I'll win."

Once again her jaw dropped before she clamped her mouth into a tight line. Obviously she knew that if he spoke with the director of nursing, Marissa's decision would be overruled. Not to mention there was also the distinct possibility that Lorraine might transfer her to another unit for the duration of Lucy's stay.

"I'm sure you would," she said quietly, "but if you stood in my shoes, wouldn't you want to be in the middle of things, too? Lucy is important to me, which is all the more reason why I *will* do whatever it takes to see her well."

"I understand but—"

"I can do this," she urged. "I know I can. Don't do this to me. Or to Lucy."

He hesitated. Lucy had always been vocal

about disliking hospitals. Given the choice, she'd want Marissa taking care of her. Hell, he'd want Marissa taking care of him, too, if he were seriously ill. But if Lucy went into convulsions or suffered other complications, he didn't want to worry about Marissa being too distraught to keep her wits about her.

"Have I ever fallen apart on you before?"

Her gaze was steady and he couldn't lie. "No."

"Then I won't this time, either."

The ER nurse halted next to the nurses' station counter. "Where do you want us?"

Marissa's gaze didn't waver from Justin's. "Room two," she told her colleague. As soon as the nurse began wheeling the gurney in the right direction, Marissa tapped her foot. "Well?"

His resolve wavered. "Okay, but if it looks like you can't handle whatever happens—"

"I'll voluntarily step aside," she finished quickly.

He studied her expression. Although he knew that Marissa had never been anything but honest, he wanted everything spelled out clearly to avoid a misunderstanding. "You're certain."

"I'm positive. Lucy's health comes first."

"No arguments?"

"No arguments," she promised.

"Then let's get to work."

Let's get to work. As if *she* were the one who'd been holding up the process, Marissa thought with exasperation as she hurried to catch up to her new patient. And yet, with each step forward, she was grateful that she'd won the battle to look after the woman who seemed more like her mother than her own.

Lucy's face appeared pale under the tan she'd already earned this spring, and her mouth was pressed into a line, as if she were in pain. She was a small woman, but Marissa never thought of her in terms of size. Her spirited personality had more than compensated for her petite frame as she puttered in her garden and engaged in enough volunteer activities to send a person half her age to bed. Right now, she hardly made a bump under the coverlet. Part of Marissa wanted to gasp in dismay, but the man she was trying to ignore would only see her reaction as a sign of weakness.

"Sorry to be such a bother." Lucy smiled wanly

as she spoke in a quivery voice that was completely unlike the vital woman Marissa had known for several years.

Marissa forced herself to act cheerfully. "No bother at all. We're here to take care of you. In the meantime, we're going to move you to a real bed, but I don't want you to do a thing. Just lie there and let us do the work."

On the count of three, they transferred Lucy carefully onto the other mattress. As soon as the ER nurse left, Marissa hurried to make Lucy as comfortable as possible with an extra pillow and warm blankets, conscious of Justin watching from his place near the foot of the bed.

As Marissa hooked Lucy to the usual monitors and checked her vital signs, she quizzed the elderly lady. "How long have you been feeling poorly? You should have said something to me last night," she chided gently, noting the woman's elevated temperature.

"It's nothing really." Lucy tried to wave her hand, then stopped, as if the motion required too much effort. "I've had a terribly bad headache that won't disappear, as well as a stiff neck that's gotten worse over the last day or so. Some nausea, too. I think it's just a bad case of the flu, although no one will listen to me." She cast a baleful glance in Justin's direction.

Marissa knew that his suspicions ran to something more serious than a touch of influenza, which was why he'd ordered the spinal tap. "We'll find out if it's the flu or not," she said cheerfully.

"I'm going to check on your lab results from the ER," Justin interrupted, "and then I'll be back. Okay?"

Lucy nodded as she closed her eyes. "I believe I'll nap in the meantime."

"Go right ahead." He met Marissa's gaze and inclined his head toward the door in a silent request for her to follow.

"Keep a close eye on her," he said in a low voice as soon as they stood in the hallway. "The ER staff reported that she seemed confused at times. You'll know better than anyone if she shows the same signs here."

Marissa nodded, feeling guilty because she hadn't noticed how sick Lucy had been the previous night. She almost said as much, but kept silent. She wouldn't give Justin any grounds for replacing her as Lucy's nurse.

Justin laid a hand on her shoulder. "It's not your fault, you know."

His uncanny perception caught her off guard. "What?"

"It's not your fault," he repeated. "Don't feel guilty that you didn't see how ill she's been."

"Who said I did?" she prevaricated.

"No one. I can tell by the look on your face." He paused. "Lucy is one of those people who suffer in silence, so don't beat yourself up for not noticing her condition. Okay?" He tipped up her chin so that her gaze met his.

"Okay," she agreed.

"Good." He sounded satisfied. "As soon as you're ready, I'll get started."

She nodded. "Give me a couple of minutes to set up." By the time she'd returned with the supplies, Justin had the latest lab report in his hand and was explaining the procedure to the elderly lady.

"It won't be very pleasant," he warned with an apologetic smile.

Lucy closed her eyes and nodded. "I'm not feeling particularly chipper right now, so anything you do will just blend in with all the other aches and pains."

He patted her forearm as he stared down at her with the compassionate gaze that Marissa had seen him give his patients so often. "We'll get to the bottom of this. I promise."

"Thank you," Lucy whispered, before her eyes glimmered with unshed tears and she sniffled. "You'll think me a silly old woman," she said in a wobbly voice that testified how strongly his conviction had touched her heart.

"You'll be weeding those petunias before long," Justin said with a wink.

A lump formed in Marissa's throat as she set the LP tray on the bedside table. She'd always dealt with her patients and their problems objectively, but it bothered her to see this seemingly unstoppable woman in such a state. Justin's fierce determination was as reassuring to her as it clearly was to Lucy. Fighting the urge to grab a tissue for herself out of the box he'd handed to his patient while knowing that if she did, she'd be sidelined before she could say "Intensive Care," she marveled at his ability to always say the right thing to his patients. Lucy wouldn't have been satisfied if he'd told her not to worry. Unlike some people, she was the sort who wanted answers, even if they weren't good, and Justin had, in effect, promised to deliver.

However, even if Lucy had been content with a platitude, her physician still wouldn't leave a stone unturned when dealing with her medical problems. Marissa wondered if his patients really knew how deeply he threw himself into their care; most probably didn't have a clue as to the lengths he went to for any one of them. If the answers weren't obvious, he spent hours researching their symptoms and contacting specialists.

Little wonder that he had no life outside the hospital. After his wife of eighteen months had packed her bags and left him on the same day he'd graduated from med school, he'd slept more often in doctors' lounges than in his own bed.

Come to think of it, he'd probably slept more often on her sofa than in his own bed, too.

"I have complete faith in you both," Lucy

said, as she blotted her eyes dry. "Now, tell me again about how you're going to poke a needle in my spine."

His raised eyebrow and pained expression as he glanced at Marissa suggested that he didn't appreciate the way Lucy had broken down his explanation. He'd obviously forgotten that age had given Lucy the right to plain speaking because, as she'd said more than once, being on the downhill slope of life meant that if she didn't speak her mind, she might never have another opportunity. At her age, she couldn't count on having a second chance to say what needed to be said.

"Actually, I'll be *sliding* the needle. Not *poking*."

Lucy waved her hand. "From where I'm sitting, it's the same difference. Either way you look at it, I've got a sharp object stuck in my back."

He chuckled. "True, but it won't be for long."

"And don't worry," Marissa came in. "Justin will make the experience as painless as possible."

"I'd appreciate it," Lucy said fervently.

Marissa gave her neighbor's hand a final squeeze, then arranged the table so that Justin's supplies would be positioned just the way he liked them. She'd worked alongside him enough times to create a routine that had become second nature. And because she didn't have to ponder his every move, she paid more attention to his conversation with his patient. He outlined everything in the right mix of medical and lay terms for Lucy to know, step by step, what would happen during the next few minutes.

As she watched Lucy visibly relax and the heart monitor reflect similar changes, she guessed that the soothing timbre of his voice was just as responsible as his matter-of-fact explanations. Although she knew that a spinal tap wasn't quite as simple as he made it sound, his voice carried such certainty and authority that even the most nervous patient's worries would have faded away.

Truthfully, though, Justin was the best of the best—even with a hand that had never fully recovered from the injuries he'd received in a plane crash—and she wasn't admitting that out of loyalty. Having seen her share of physicians whose skill ranged from the average to the exceptional, she knew in which physician she'd place her complete trust. Lucy couldn't have asked for anyone better.

"If those are all of your questions," Justin said, signaling Marissa to move Lucy into a recumbent position with her back toward him, "we'll get started."

"All right, but I think you're making too much fuss over a headache and a stiff neck," Lucy grumbled, although her tone lacked any spark of conviction. "I only came to the ER to get stronger pain relief."

"Taking care of my patients isn't making a fuss," Justin remarked as he donned his sterile gloves.

"How long have you felt like this?" Marissa asked, aware that Lucy had evaded her earlier question. Three days ago, Lucy had been puttering among her flowers and although Marissa had only waved and chatted with her over the fence for a few minutes the previous night, Lucy had seemed fine.

"About a week."

"A week?" Marissa was horrified. Her guilt for not noticing Lucy's deterioration grew to epic proportions until it threatened to choke her. "And you didn't say anything?"

"Oh, dearie. When you get to my age, you try to ignore as much as you can. Why, if I called you or ran to the doctor every time I had an ache or a pain, I'd be wearing out the furniture in Justin's waiting room."

"I wish you would wear out those chairs," he replied as his sidelong glance at Marissa reminded her of their earlier conversation about not feeling guilty. "My waiting room needs a face-lift," he continued.

"A face-lift?" Marissa echoed. "Wow. I can't believe you actually admitted it."

"I'm not completely oblivious to my sur-roundings," he said defensively. "Pea-green chairs and gold wallpaper aren't exactly soothing colors to healthy people, much less sick ones."

Marissa stared at him in awe. "You actually notice things like that?"

"Of course I do, but if you're going to start nagging me again about how it's time I paint my house and buy matching furniture…" His voice held a warning note.

"Why would I do that?" she asked innocently

as she mentally added neckties to the list. "Every time I mention it, my suggestion falls on deaf ears, so I won't waste my breath." For the last few years, she'd tried to convince him to put his own stamp on the house he'd bought when he'd moved to Hope. A man of his standing in the community needed more than a bed and a dresser, a kitchen table with two chairs and a sofa courtesy of someone's garage sale. But, as he liked to remind her, he spent more time at the hospital and her house than his, so what did he care if his walls were bare and he didn't fill every nook and cranny with furniture?

"Good idea."

While Justin raised the bed to the right height for him to work, Marissa helped Lucy draw her knees to her abdomen and flex her neck before she covered her exposed back with a sterile drape.

"This may be cold." Justin prepped the skin over Lucy's spine with antiseptic-soaked, cotton-tipped applicators.

Lucy's sharp intake of breath suggested that she agreed. "I really don't want to think about what you're doing," she began, "so to keep my mind off the idea of your using me as a pin cushion, I want to chat."

"What about?" Justin asked.

"The flowers."

"Flowers?" Marissa asked absentmindedly as she tried to anticipate Justin's needs. "Your petunias look wonderful."

"Not those. I'm asking about the ones in the nurses' station."

"Oh." Marissa was beginning to hate flowers or any mention thereof. "Those."

"Yes, those. I caught the distinct scent of roses, even though I didn't see any."

Marissa inwardly sighed. Travis's actions may have been sweet, but they were certainly causing quite a stir. "We did have roses earlier," she admitted, "but they aren't here anymore."

"Ah," Lucy said, a satisfied set on her face. "I thought so. I may be old, but my nose still works perfectly."

"Actually," Justin added smoothly as he injected lidocaine into the area around Lucy's spine, "Marissa got all sorts of flowers. It was quite exciting. Wasn't it, Mari?"

She frowned at him, wishing she could tell him to stuff a sock in it. If she wanted to discuss the meaning behind the flowers with Lucy—and she did—she'd rather do so without an audience. But he'd brought it up and now she had no choice….

Justin raised an eyebrow as he waited for Marissa to explain the details. He wasn't particularly eager to address the issue of those blasted flowers because he had a feeling that he wouldn't like what he'd hear, but if the conversation kept Lucy's mind off what he was doing, then he'd suffer through it.

Maybe he was also a glutton for punishment, because he wanted to know exactly what had prompted Mr. Money Bags to set his sights on Marissa. Travis Pendleton didn't seem the type to be interested in a working girl, not when rumors abounded that moving out of the city manager's position in the small town of Hope and into a similar job in a major metropolitan area was the first stop on his goal to reach the state senate. A fashion model or a business tycoon's daughter seemed more his style.

"Seven bouquets showed up for me today,"

Marissa admitted as her cheeks turned a dusky pink. "They came as quite a…um, surprise."

Justin thought it odd that she almost sounded pained to claim them. Most women would have been floating three feet off the ground under similar circumstances, and he was curious why Marissa seemed almost embarrassed by the gesture. Then again, Pendleton probably hadn't figured out that Marissa didn't like to draw attention to herself. If the man had possessed any inkling of Marissa's character, he would have known seven was overkill. Unfortunately, discussing the man's short-comings would have to wait until he had finished with Lucy. He simply couldn't afford to let his attention wander too far off the mark.

At one time, he could have gone through the motions of this procedure with his eyes closed. However, ever since he'd broken his hand in the plane crash that had killed one of Hope's physicians and injured a few others, it had taken a lot of physical therapy to get to the point where he could even perform a spinal tap. While he was pleased that he'd regained eighty percent of his preaccident dexterity, he hated that he still hadn't reached the hundred percent mark. Lucy, or any other patient, didn't deserve to have a physician who couldn't perform at peak efficiency. If he didn't carry out this procedure flawlessly, he could do lasting damage.

As if aware of the stress he'd placed himself under, his hand cramped as he picked up the needle off the sterile supply tray and it slid out of his stiff fingers. Fortunately, it landed back on the sterile tray and not on the floor.

For an instant he stared at the scene, aware of Marissa hovering nearby. To her credit, she didn't cast a pitying glance at him, like so many other nurses would have. Neither did she suggest that he step aside for someone else.

He flexed his right hand to ease the cramp as he met her steady gaze. The faith in her green eyes and the smile on her Cupid's-bow mouth gave him the confidence boost he needed.

Heaving a wordless sigh, he picked up the needle again with his gloved fingers and hefted it in his hand. He could do this. He *would* do this.

As soon as the needle went into the subarachnoid space with a satisfying pop, he relaxed.

Unbidden, his attention returned to Marissa, whose wide smile and thumbs-up sign was more than enough reward.

"They must be from that young man who came by last night." Lucy's comment drew him back to the conversation.

"They are," Marissa confirmed as her pixielike face turned a darker shade of pink and highlighted her cheekbones.

"What a nice gesture. He's certainly thoughtful."

"Yes, he is."

Justin wanted to point out that if Travis was as thoughtful as they believed, he wouldn't have sent more flowers than some people received at their funerals. Neither would he have sent them to a unit where flowers weren't permitted and where the potential of causing problems for Marissa was so great.

"I noticed he held the car door for you," Lucy commented.

"Why, Lucy, were you watching me?" Marissa sounded horrified, which rankled Justin. Just what had they been doing that she hadn't wanted Lucy, or anyone else, to see?

"Of course, dear. One can't be too careful about strangers arriving in the neighborhood. He has exquisite manners, which is quite unusual in this day and age."

"Yes, it is," Marissa agreed.

Manners. Justin frowned. What was it with women? They claimed to want independence and all that, but then they got all gooey-eyed because someone helped them with their coat or opened a door. Men simply couldn't win. They were damned if they did, and damned if they didn't. He knew because his wife—his *ex-wife*—had taught him that particular lesson well.

Even so, he'd spent enough time with Marissa over the years to know that he hadn't treated her like one of the guys. He may not have been overly attentive, but he *had* put his mother's teachings to good use.

"I wouldn't say that holding doors open for a date is so unusual," he said as he removed the stylet and spinal fluid dripped out of the needle and into the collection tubes. The fluid was clear and not cloudy or bloody, which came as a relief.

"You'd be surprised," Marissa said grimly.

While he didn't believe Travis, the Wonder Date, had actually done anything out of the ordinary, it didn't hurt to find out exactly what had impressed them. One never knew what piece of trivial information might come in handy, not that he intended to put it to use anytime soon.

"What do women expect from men these days?" he asked.

"My goodness, Justin," Lucy said weakly, although her surprise was still obvious, "don't tell me you've forgotten how to court a lady."

"I haven't forgotten," he protested. "I date on occasion."

"Oh, really?" Marissa sounded skeptical and she had every right to be. Medicine and his patients came first in his life and he only fit in the odd date or two on the fringes. He usually spent his spare time playing basketball with the guys at the gym or watching movies at Marissa's.

"Really," he affirmed. "I went to the Valentine's Day ball with a date. Cam proposed to Dixie, remember? And before that was the annual hospital Christmas party. Don't forget the end of harvest festival coming up in August. I always bring a guest to that."

"Three dates in a year?" Lucy asked, incredulous. "No wonder you're still single."

"I'm positive I've gone out more than three times," he protested. "I just can't remember them. In any case, it doesn't hurt to hear what women expect. What, exactly, did Trent do?"

"Travis," Marissa corrected.

He shrugged. "Whatever. It rained last night, so I suppose he spread his coat across a puddle to keep your shoes from getting wet."

"No, but he had an umbrella."

Considering the weather forecast hadn't given decent odds for moisture, he was marginally impressed. "A regular Boy Scout."

"Jealous?"

He glanced at her to see the question in her green eyes that reminded him of sparkling emeralds. "Hardly. Although I thought you liked to walk in the rain."

He hadn't planned to sound accusatory, but somehow he had. Probably because he could remember several Saturday afternoons when the two of them had ambled along the park's walking path during a heavy drizzle just so she could enjoy the fresh air. He'd agreed, not because he enjoyed getting soaked down to his skivvies but because there had been something so childlike about the experience. Revisiting his childhood wasn't something he did often, but once in a while the stress of his profession got to be over-whelming. For the length of those walks he could forget that he held people's lives in his hands, that some people simply couldn't be saved.

"I do when I'm dressed for the occasion, but not when I'm wearing a dress and heels."

She had a point.

"You know, dear," Lucy interjected, "your Travis sounds wonderful. Did you have a good time?"

She didn't hesitate. "Yes."

"Is he the one?"

Justin's ears perked as he waited for her answer. The fact that she hesitated meant that she had doubts or at least some reservations.

Reservations were good. If he'd listened to his inner warnings about Chandra, he could have avoided a heap of trouble in his life. As Marissa's friend for many years, he was bound and determined to save her some grief, if he could.

"It's too soon to tell," she finished smoothly.

He let out the breath he'd been holding.

"Don't rush into anything," Lucy said in a far-away voice. "I know you aren't getting younger and people like to talk about a woman's biological clock ticking, but it doesn't hurt to be positively sure about a decision."

"Here, here!" Justin chimed in, refusing to let Marissa's glare intimidate him.

"Although," Lucy continued as if he hadn't spoken, "I've never been able to understand why you two have never gotten together."

"We *are* together." Marissa sounded puzzled. "I met Travis a few weeks ago."

"Not him. You and Justin."

Justin nearly swallowed his tongue. From Marissa's sudden intake of breath, he knew she'd experienced the same reaction. "Us?" she squeaked.

Us? he echoed in his mind. Where would Lucy get an idea like that?

And yet the idea didn't send him recoiling in

horror. Yes, they spent several evenings a week in each other's company and had ever since he'd moved to Hope and discovered that Marissa lived here, too. They'd also gone to dinner and the movies whenever a new film had come to town, but those had always been platonic outings. More often than not, they went Dutch, although there had been a few times when he'd left his billfold in his scrub suit at the hospital and Mari had paid for their hamburgers and movie tickets.

But he'd always paid her back. Hadn't he? He frowned, trying to recall the circumstances, then decided they didn't matter. What was more important was understanding how Lucy had jumped to her conclusion.

"What made you think that?" he asked, curious to hear her answer.

"You spend a lot of time together," Lucy said, clearly oblivious to the charged atmosphere swirling around the two people in question. "Look at how often you see each other at the hospital. And don't forget all those evenings you drop by Marissa's house. Don't deny it because I see your car parked outside several times a week."

Lucy was right. Why had he never noticed how his "official" dates were scheduled into his life like appointments with his physical therapist, but he saw Marissa more often than not? While he was shocked and surprised by the notion, the mental picture it generated didn't horrify him.

Not one bit.

"We're just friends, Lucy. Justin isn't my type." Her firm tone couldn't have made her opinion more clear. As far as she was concerned, the idea plainly fell beyond all realm of possibility.

Instead of feeling reassured, his ego bristled. Just what type did she think he *was*?

While they didn't necessarily like the same things—he preferred coffee over her tea; she liked golf while he was happier playing basketball or football; she favored spicy foods while they gave him heartburn—they got along well. They might have differing opinions, but he always felt as if he could say what he thought without worrying if he would offend her. From their rousing discussions, he'd hazard to say that she did the same.

But if she thought that smooth-talking snake-oil salesman Travis Pendleton was more her type than *he* was, then he would definitely have to work hard to convince her of how wrong she was.

"And I'm not his type, either," she added firmly. "If it weren't for us both being in health care, we'd have nothing in common."

Nothing in common? He wanted to protest, but Lucy beat him to the punch.

"Nonsense. Differences are good." Lucy's words slurred. "Don't forget how well you both connect with each other. You've laid a strong foundation and it's a shame you two haven't built anything on it."

"I think you're suffering from an overactive imagination," Marissa stated kindly to her neighbor. "We're only good friends. Even if we weren't, Justin is a die-hard bachelor, so you're wasting your time at playing matchmaker. Isn't that right, Doctor?"

Her description stung. A bachelor, yes, but *die-hard*? Not particularly. He might prefer to keep his relationships simple and uncomplicated, but

Marissa's version made him seem so...inflexible and stubborn, not to mention lonely.

Contrary to what people might believe, he wanted the same things that every other man wanted—a cozy house and a warm wife. The problem was that he'd chosen poorly the first time and he dreaded a repeat of his mistake.

He would have explained his reluctance to Lucy, but he was ready to wrap up both the procedure and the conversation that reminded him of lost dreams.

"Okay, Lucy, we're done." Justin removed the needle from her spine and pressed a pad of gauze to the site. A sense of relief swept over him for accomplishing the task without another mishap. He'd officially scaled one more obstacle in his own healing process. As long as his good days outnumbered the bad ones, he intended to prove the specialist wrong. He'd already progressed further than initially expected.

"Really? Now, that wasn't so awful," Lucy said. "I'll have to be sure and tell Morris that he's been worrying over nothing. He's such a sweet husband, always fretting about me."

Knowing that Lucy had been a widow for at least ten years, he raised a questioning eyebrow at Marissa, who responded with a puzzled shrug.

"He's waiting outside, you know," Lucy added dreamily.

Marissa frowned. "Lucy," she said hesitantly. "Your husband isn't outside. He's…"

"Oh, that's right. He went to the garden store because I need food for my roses, fertilizer for my flowers and mosquito spray. With all the moisture we've had, those pesky insects are quite bad this year. If you don't mind, I'm rather tired and I'd like to sleep now.

"And don't you two worry about me," Lucy added, as if sensing their concern. "Morris says I'm going to be just fine."

At a sudden loss for words—what would it hurt if remembering her husband gave her comfort?—Justin exchanged a final helpless glance with Marissa before he moved to a corner of the room to record his notes and lab orders. As he scribbled on the pages, he listened with half an ear to Marissa's soft voice cautioning Lucy to lie quietly for at least an hour. From the older woman's condition, he suspected Lucy would do so even without Marissa's advice.

"I want the usual cell counts, glucose and protein and culture," he said as soon as Marissa joined him in the hallway. "I also want blood drawn for a West Nile virus test. And call me as soon as you have those results."

"West Nile?" she asked, clearly surprised by his request.

"'Tis the season," he quoted. "It's early, I know, but when she mentioned mosquitoes, I thought of it."

"I'll call as soon as I hear from the lab, but the West Nile test will take a couple of days." She paused. "I'm a little surprised that she talked as if her husband was still alive."

"Me, too. Keep a close eye on her," he said as he handed over the medical record.

"I will."

His gaze landed on the pot of flowers remaining on the nurses' counter and his mouth tightened in displeasure. He didn't know why Mr. City Manager's exorbitant display irritated him so much. If Pendleton wanted to spend hundreds of dollars on flowers, who was he to stop him from supporting the local economy? Yet irritate him it did.

His irritation only grew when he saw the arrangement in Newland's room, although he didn't show it. But by the time he'd examined Newland and talked to his wife, he was well and truly sick of flowers.

To add insult to injury, the sight of Marissa at the nurses' station only reminded him of Lucy's comments. "Call if anything changes," he said more gruffly than necessary, before he disappeared into the nearby stairwell to escape the sweet aroma saturating the ICU. Unfortunately, he couldn't escape the memory of Lucy's words.

I've never understood why you two have never gotten together.... Don't forget how well you connect with each other...a strong foundation...

Contrary to what Lucy thought, he knew exactly what they had. Their friendship had started on the first day of his French I class, when he'd slid into the chair next to a brown-haired girl with hazel eyes that turned deeper shades of blue or green, depending on her mood. She'd quietly listened during the lecture and acted as if she understood every word the professor had said, while he'd been completely lost.

Marissa had helped him pass the course and throughout the rest of the semester he'd discovered that not only was she intelligent and possessed a soft heart, but she was also a good listener. Their mutual interest in medicine had cemented their friendship, although his path had led to med school and hers into nursing.

They had exchanged Christmas cards at that point, although his had been the e-mail variety and usually late. Those annual contacts had gradually dwindled and finally ended once he'd married Chandra Weaver. It was only after they'd both reconnected in Hope several years ago after his divorce that they'd caught up on each other's lives. Since then, it had seemed as if they'd never been separated.

What surprised him the most was Marissa's single status—waiting, as she said, for the right man. Were the eligible fellows blind? But whether they were or not, he didn't want her to make his same mistakes, so he did his best to keep a watchful eye on her prospects. It hadn't been too difficult because in a town this size, everyone knew everyone else's business.

Unfortunately, Travis Pendleton wasn't a home-grown boy. He was a new arrival and although people in his circles spoke favorably of him, if something was too good to be true, it usually was.

Normally, he wouldn't worry about Marissa being taken in by a handsome face or sappy romantic gestures, but now he wasn't so sure. She hadn't actually confirmed that she and Terrific Trevor were an item, but she hadn't denied it, either. She'd simply declared that Pendleton was a friend, but that was how she described *him*, too.

Something about the situation was…unsettling. Yes, that was the word. Unsettling. He had never considered himself a creature of habit or a person who resisted change, but he didn't want to rock the current boat when it was sailing along quite nicely.

And yet….his internal early warning system suggested that change was in the wind.

Impulsively, he reversed direction and bounded back up the stairs. Fortunately, he found Marissa working alone in their small medication room.

"Do you have plans tonight?" he asked without preamble.

She looked up from her supply list. "Back so soon?"

"Do you have plans tonight?" he repeated.

"Yes, I do. Why?"

"Change them."

She stared at him as if he'd grown two heads. "Hardly," she retorted. "Travis is coming over."

"What time?"

"After his meeting ends. Probably around nine."

"Then I'll be there at eight."

A worried wrinkle appeared on her brow. "Is something wrong?"

Hell, yes, there was something wrong. The problem was, he didn't know what it was.

Actually, he did know. He didn't like the idea of Marissa keeping company with a man who was, as far as he was concerned, completely wrong for her. Pendleton and Marissa traveled in two different circles and forcing them into one was a situation that spelled disaster.

"I'll come over at eight," he repeated.

"What for?" she asked, wary.

If he admitted that he wanted to warn her about rushing into a relationship, she'd probably tie his stethoscope into a knot—around his neck. He quickly cast for another excuse and reeled it in. "To talk about us."

Her eyes widened in surprise, then cleared as she shook her head. "There is no 'us,' Justin. We're friends and have been for a long time."

"Lucy doesn't think so—"

"Oh, for heaven's sake," she interrupted crossly. "It doesn't matter what Lucy thinks. As much as I love her, she sees what she wants to see. She might believe that we'd make the perfect couple, but if it hasn't happened by now, it isn't going to happen. So don't give it another thought."

A long pause followed as he pondered why her outright refusal to try Lucy's comment on for size disappointed him. He at least was willing to consider the possibilities before deciding yea or nay. But if Marissa wasn't open to the idea, then there wasn't any point, was there?

"As long as we're both on the same page," he said slowly. "No misunderstandings."

"Believe me, there aren't any," she said pointedly. "Our situation couldn't be clearer if it were spelled out in marquee lights. Now, if you're finished, I have work to do." Immediately, she turned her attention back to the paper in her hand.

Another man would have taken her at face value, but he swore—*swore*—that she'd sounded strange, even wistful, which didn't make any sense at all.

"OK, but I'm still coming over at eight."

Her startled gaze met his. "What for?"

"We've always been honest with each other," he reminded her. "Haven't we?"

"Yes." She sounded cautious.

"You can tell me all about Travis."

She folded her arms. "You won't listen."

"I will. I promise."

"Before or after you warn me to look before I leap? To check him out thoroughly? To take things slow?"

"Okay, okay. I'll listen before I say a word. The point is, he didn't do the flower thing out of the goodness of his heart. The guy's after something." Sex, most likely, he grumbled to himself.

"Thank you for that insight," she muttered. "If you're trying to warn me, you're too late."

His protective instincts erupted like Mt. St. Helens. "Don't tell me you've already slept with him."

Surprise instantly appeared on her face, only to be replaced a second later by cool disdain. "Whether I did or didn't doesn't concern you, Justin. I already know what he wants."

"You do?" He paused, waiting for her to explain herself, but when she didn't, he pressed on. "You can't keep me hanging, Marissa."

She faced him squarely. "If you must know this very moment, I'll tell you." Her pause lasted only the length of a heartbeat. "He wants me to marry him."

CHAPTER THREE

MARISSA wondered what mischievous imp had taken control of her tongue and allowed her to blurt out that half-truth. Yes, she'd wanted to shock him, surprise Justin, and get him to lighten up on his big-brother routine, but she'd never imagined that she'd render him completely speechless and looking like a landed trout.

If she truly wanted to make him suffer, she'd walk away and let him stew until that evening, but she couldn't risk the start of any rumors. Now, as the seconds stretched out, she wished she'd chosen her words more carefully. She didn't believe in bad luck or jinxes, but the situation with Travis was still too new and too tenuous for her to start shopping for wedding gowns or to allow people to think she was.

"He proposed?" he asked before she could find the right words to retract her statement.

"Yes and no."

"You can't have it both ways, Mari. He either did or he didn't."

As much as she wanted to clear the air, she hated having to explain this. "If you must know, we discussed marriage, but only in general terms."

"Then he didn't propose."

She didn't understand his utter look of relief. After all, what difference should it make to him? "Technically, no. As I mentioned, we were talking and—"

"About what?"

She frowned at his clipped tone. "About everything—families, settling down, kids, etcetera. Then he commented on how well we got along after such a short time of knowing each other and that we should think about tying the knot someday."

Travis had spoken lightheartedly, and she'd responded in kind, but it had to be a good sign if he was already thinking, however remotely, along the lines of a committed relationship.

"Someday."

"Yes, someday. Although, to be honest, it wouldn't surprise me if 'someday' isn't very far in the future." She hoped.

"Rushing things a bit, aren't you?"

"I'm not rushing at all. He hasn't asked and I haven't answered," she reminded him. "As I said, we're in the early stages of our relationship. So I don't want you meddling or interfering in any way."

"Me, meddle or interfere?"

"Don't look so innocent, Justin. You know I'm right."

"I don't meddle," he said, clearly affronted. "I only act as a sounding board, as your voice of reason."

"Well, stifle it," she ordered. "This could be a good thing for me and I don't want you mucking it up in any way, shape or form. And that means no internet credit checks, no trying to hunt down past girlfriends or previous employers, *nothing*."

"But, Mari—"

"I'm serious. *Nothing*. I'm a big girl and can make up my own mind. If I want your opinion, I'll ask for it."

He frowned, then replaced it with a look of resignation. "Okay."

"Good. Then it's settled."

He turned to leave, then stopped. "If he did propose, would you say yes?"

He was certainly tenacious, she had to admit. "Now who's rushing things?"

"Just answer my question, Mari. Would you accept?"

Mari stared at the man she'd known for nearly twelve years. The same man who popped into her fantasies during weak moments. The same man who would have made her the happiest woman alive if he'd ever noticed her as a woman and not just as "one of the guys." It was so very easy to picture him seated across an intimate table for two, complete with roses and candlelight, as he placed a tiny velvet box in her hand.

But that would never happen. The years had marched on and she'd learned one important thing during her twenty-nine years on this earth—it was futile to wait for the impossible or the improbable.

She fisted her hands to stop herself from

tracing the hard lines of his face. She'd never allowed herself to touch him other than in a most impersonal way, and she mourned the loss, but some things in life just weren't meant to be. She couldn't afford to be foolish and wait for romantic sparks to appear from nowhere.

Would she accept Travis's proposal if one came along?

"Yes," she said quietly. "Yes, I would."

"What are you doing here?" Marissa whispered angrily when she saw Justin standing in the night-time shadows on her porch.

"Sorry, I'm late," he said without a single note of true apology in his voice as he picked up an excited Toby and scratched behind the Cairn terrier's ears. "Sick patient."

"I already have company," she ground out.

He winked. "I don't mind."

"Well, I do," she retorted. "You were supposed to be here at eight. It's almost ten."

"Can I help it if duty called first?"

"No," she grumbled, aware that when he was on call, he usually did get called. "Although I don't know why you bothered to come at all. Didn't we cover everything earlier today?"

"Yeah, but you can't blame me for wanting to meet the guy who has you all aflutter, can you?"

"Oh, I suppose not," she said grudgingly. "Does it have to be today, though?"

"No time like the present."

She grabbed Toby and tucked him under her arm. "Okay, but you can't stay long." Inviting Travis into her home for the first time had been nerve-racking enough, without worrying what Justin might say or do.

"I won't. Wouldn't want to interfere in the course of true love." He winked again.

Marissa rolled her eyes. "And you won't give him the third degree?"

He held up three fingers. "I solemnly swear."

"All right, then. Let's get this over with. Just remember. Five minutes and you'll leave."

"Sure thing, Mari."

"Wait here while I put Toby in his kennel."

"You're kenneling Toby? What's he done?" He grinned. "Carried your panties out of the bedroom while company was here?"

"Thank goodness, no." Knowing how Toby liked to chew on silk, she'd made sure all her underwear lay out of Toby's canine reach. "Travis isn't fond of dogs."

Justin rubbed the Cairn's head. "Not fond of this heart-breaker? Impossible."

"Yeah, well, the feeling is mutual. Toby's been grumbling at him ever since he walked through the door."

"Interesting."

She wasn't going to admit to Justin that she was disappointed by the lack of rapport between her pet and her boyfriend.

"He probably just doesn't like Travis's cologne," she said defensively.

"Could be." He reached for Toby. "Give him to me. He'll behave."

She hesitated. All she needed was for her dog to send Travis running for the hills. She'd been afraid of what Justin would do, but hadn't considered Toby causing problems, too. "Are you sure?"

"Is ice skating an Olympic event?"

"All right, but if he growls just once, he's taking time out in his kennel."

"Yes, ma'am." He ruffled Toby's fur. "Hear that, buddy? The boss has spoken. We both have to be on our best behavior."

Toby answered by licking Justin's chin.

Travis's first visit was turning out better and better, she thought glumly. Leading the way into her living room, with Toby trotting happily beside Justin, she performed the introductions. They shook hands and retreated to opposite sides of the room, like boxers going to their respective corners.

How odd that she would see their actions in that way. She hoped it wouldn't indicate how the next few minutes would go. If she had her way, though, Justin would be gone in less time than it took to take a blood pressure.

Determined to hurry her momentarily unwelcome guest home before he said something she would regret, she grabbed the DVD lying on the coffee table.

"Justin stopped by to borrow a movie," she said as she passed it to him without looking. "Here you go. Happy viewing."

Justin didn't take the hint to leave. Instead, he

sank into an easy chair and motioned for Toby to jump into his lap before he glanced at the title. And grinned.

"Just what I wanted to see," he said as he scratched behind the Cairn's ears. "*Casanova*. Nothing like a good chick flick to cure insomnia. Thanks, Mari."

She'd given him *Casanova*? Travis would either see through Justin's flimsy excuse for dropping by and realize that he was being checked out or wonder what sort of man Dr. St. James actually was. It would serve Justin right if Travis thought he was gay.

"If you want a different movie…"

"No, no," he said, shaking his head. "This one's fine."

To Marissa's dismay, he leaned back in the chair as if settling in for a long visit. "What do you think about the Cubs' chance to win the pennant this year?"

"My money's on the Yankees," Travis replied.

"They're a good team," Justin admitted. "I'd like to see someone else on top for a change."

While the two discussed the ins and outs of

professional baseball, Marissa took a moment to study them.

Travis was light to Justin's dark. He had blue eyes and sandy-colored hair that even at this time of night lay in perfect order. Justin's hair, on the other hand, was tousled, as if he'd run his hands through it a few times.

Justin had obviously gone home at some point because he'd traded his blue shirt, black slacks and dress shoes for faded blue jeans, a red T-shirt and scuffed tennis shoes. He might look like a successful physician between eight and five, but after that comfort—not style—dictated his choice of attire. As far as she knew, no one seemed to mind that he looked more like Mr. July on a handyman pin-up calendar than a doctor. The patients were usually too ill and too grateful for his services after normal office hours to care. As for the staff, most of the nurses prayed for a reason to see those luscious buns encased in snug-fitting denim.

On the other hand, Travis still wore his dark blue suit, which wasn't surprising as he'd come directly from work to her house. The only concession to the time was his slightly loosened silk tie, which had probably cost as much as his suit. Idly, she wondered if she'd ever see Travis wearing anything except business clothes but, then, he *was* a public figure in the community and clearly dressed the part. For a man who planned to move to the top, appearances were everything.

While both men were handsome, Justin's dark coloring was more of a turn-on to her than Travis's lighter complexion, and she immediately chided herself for the disloyal thought. A man's character was more important than his looks. Travis's fairness aside, he was an attractive, thoughtful man.

"How are things down at City Hall?"

Justin's question pulled her out of her daydream. They'd obviously had a congenial conversation because she couldn't detect any undercurrents of tension. Thank goodness. Maybe, just maybe, this wouldn't turn out as horribly as she had feared.

"Busy," Travis replied. "We're in the business of preparing our next fiscal year's budget. As I was telling Marissa, I'll be crunching numbers for the next few weeks."

"Really?" Justin appeared interested as he stroked Toby's soft fur. "You don't just adjust last year's figures to cover increased expenses and inflation?"

"Oh, it's far more complicated than that," he said airily. "I'm going through every line item to determine its importance. It's crucial for the city to set aside funds for those rainy-day expenses and to do that, we have to cut out the waste. But, then, you probably don't do that with your medical practice, do you?"

"To a certain extent we do," Justin admitted mildly. "Medicine is becoming more of a business all the time. With insurance issues, federal regulations and reimbursements, it's sometimes difficult to find the happy medium between going into debt and providing good-quality health care."

"Unfortunately, the city doesn't have your same luxury of being able to raise office fees to cover any shortfalls."

Marissa heard the challenge in Travis's voice and mentally cringed. Most people didn't realize just how strongly Justin felt about the high cost of health care. He took great pains to keep prices down for his patients and often treated his poor, uninsured patients for pennies on the dollar. To hear someone's general assumption that physicians cared little about finances was bound to strike off a few of his sparks. Before she could interject a defense on his behalf, Justin responded.

"Actually, our fees are based on current reimbursement rates," Justin said in the specificly mild tone that signaled the complete opposite to those who knew him. "In my practice, we don't set those arbitrarily. And if we did, that would be as popular a move as when the government, whether it's city, county, state or federal, increases our taxes to raise more money."

Travis nodded. "It's difficult for people to accept having to pay more for the same service, but it's often a fact of life."

At that moment Toby rolled onto his back as his way of begging for a tummy rub. Justin chuckled as he obliged. "Beggar," he teased. "Say, Travis, has Toby performed any of his tricks for you?"

Marissa momentarily relaxed as the tense moment eased.

"No," Travis answered.

"Too bad. Toby's a smart dog. If you feed him a few Cheerios, he'll be your friend for life." He scratched the sandy-colored Cairn's tummy harder. "Won't you, buddy?"

"Travis isn't fond of dogs," Marissa mentioned, wishing she'd sat close enough to Justin to deliver a warning kick to his shins.

"I like dogs," Travis corrected. "I just don't believe they belong indoors. No offense, Marissa. It's a personal preference thing."

"I understand." Surely, given time, her well-behaved Toby would win him over.

Travis stretched his long legs and crossed his ankles. "The ones that really drive me crazy are the ones that yip at anything and everything."

"Toby doesn't yip," Justin said. "He's been a great watchdog for Marissa, which is good for a woman living alone."

"True, but a state-of-the-art security system doesn't shed hair on the furniture."

"It doesn't curl up beside you at night, either," Marissa said.

"No, but I can think of something better than a four-legged fur ball to curl up with at night."

As Travis directed his lazy grin in Marissa's direction, the promise in his eyes made his thoughts all too plain. Heat crept up Marissa's neck but rather than feel embarrassed, she was glad Justin had witnessed the exchange. She'd always wanted her old friend to see her as an attractive woman but he hadn't. Maybe Travis's blatant hint would open his eyes, because he'd have to be blind and deaf to miss the other man's interest. She couldn't have planned it better.

She stole a glance in Justin's direction, but he seemed far more engrossed in Toby than in Travis's comments. Disappointed, she let out a deep breath. Better luck next time, she vowed.

Justin had never considered himself a violent man, but right now he was itching to punch Pendleton's face. What was he thinking of to give Marissa a blatant invitation to sleep together, and in front of a complete stranger? And both Lucy and Marissa thought the man held the corner on the manners market. Hah!

The man certainly was proud of himself and his job, Justin decided. He wondered if Marissa had heard the nuances of their conversation and recognized Travis's one-upmanship for what it was.

He flexed his fingers, wishing he could send Pendleton packing. If the man made another inappropriate comment, he would.

Toby suddenly squeaked and shifted positions as he stared up at Justin with confusion in his doggy eyes. Realizing he'd painfully pulled the dog's hair, he straightened his fingers and patted the dog's tummy. "Sorry, Toby," he murmured. "I didn't mean to take it out on you."

Toby rolled onto his stomach, laid his head on Justin's forearm and wore his most forlorn expression, as if he understood Justin's frustrations. Perhaps he did. It certainly didn't take a high IQ to deduce that Toby's days with Marissa were numbered if Pendleton stayed in the picture. Barring a move to a new owner, Toby would be living in her backyard, looking in.

Toby wouldn't be the only one relegated to second-class citizen status. Justin would be there, too. Even if he remained friends with Marissa, their time together would be similar to the evening he was enduring now. He'd be the third wheel, the odd man out, the one who would go home alone while they would have each other. Pendleton would be the one to enjoy Marissa's long legs wrapped around him. *He* would sink into her velvety softness, see her shining smile, soothe her hurts and listen to her confidences.

Couldn't she see that while Pendleton might be a decent sort, his attitude toward Toby proved that he wasn't right for her?

And who was?

Justin didn't know, but he was certain that it wasn't Pendleton. As he covertly studied her face and the blush that the other man had put there, Justin thought of a dozen reasons why he should mind his own business and only one why he should not. Logically, those reasons overruled his desire to interfere, but suddenly it didn't matter if he had only one or a hundred justifiable motives to meddle. His single excuse overshadowed all others.

If Marissa chose to spend her life with Pendleton, Justin's life would change forever, too. And he wasn't ready for that to happen.

* * *

"What have you done to yourself?" Marissa exclaimed as soon as Justin walked into the ICU the next morning.

"Nothing, why?"

"You look terrible."

"Really?" He tiredly rubbed the back of his neck. "My mirror told me I was quite presentable."

"You are," she said. "Your hair is combed, you're clean-shaven and your clothes are pressed, but you must have been awake all night."

"And I thought I didn't have circles under my eyes."

"You don't," she said. "You're one of those lucky people who doesn't get circles or bags under his eyes."

"Then how can you tell when no one else can?"

"There's something about your expression—I can't explain it. I suppose it's a combination of your smile not seeming as bright or as relaxed as usual and your eyes aren't as sparkly and cantankerous."

"Cantankerous? Thanks for making me sound like I'm ninety-five," he said wryly.

"Okay, okay. Make that 'lively' instead."

"Lively is good."

She smiled. "I'm glad you approve. What kept you out all night? You left my house at eleven. Couldn't sleep?"

"Believe me, it wasn't because I didn't want to. Let's see." He ticked his reasons off on his hand. "The uncontrolled diabetic, which as you know, was early in the evening. Then I had the possible MI when I was at your place."

He'd been paged while Travis had been expounding on his vintage wine collection and instructing them on the finer points of winemaking. Travis definitely did not consider any wine that cost less than three hundred dollars a bottle worth drinking. Justin had nearly mentioned that Marissa's favorite brand cost only a fraction of that, but stopped himself. Embarrassing her in front of someone she wanted to impress would be counterproductive.

"By the way," he asked, "did Toby behave after I left?"

"More or less. He sat on my lap and pouted until Travis left around midnight. He doesn't like it when people don't pay attention to him."

"He's a ham," Justin agreed. "Toby likes

people and can't understand why someone wouldn't like him, too. No wonder the poor dog grumbled at Travis."

"Toby'll have to get used to it. I can't blame Travis for not wanting dog hair on his suit, though."

"A fate worse than death," he agreed facetiously.

She glared, which only meant that his sarcasm hadn't gone over her head. "You were talking about why you were gone all night?"

"Oh, yeah. After the MI, I had a fellow who's blood pressure was high enough for a stroke, so we watched him. Then I had a guy come in with a nosebleed that wouldn't quit, so I had to pack his nose, and—"

"Where were the ER docs? Dr. Tremaine or Dr. Stafford?"

"Jared was on duty but he was busy with a car wreck. Five people injured with four needing surgery. I hung around to handle the minor stuff as most of them were my patients anyway."

He may have been physically occupied with tending patients all night, but that hadn't stopped his mind from occasionally wandering to Marissa. Luckily he'd been too busy with patients to dwell on what she and Pendleton were doing at her house, although at two a.m. he'd fought the strongest urge to drive by her house. Now he took comfort that it hadn't been necessary.

Equally fortunate was how Toby had done his part at keeping those two from tangoing between the sheets. He made a mental note to buy the year-old Cairn a case of his favorite beef-and-cheese treats.

"Isn't that what you always do?" she asked. "Hang around the ER to help out? I'll bet the docs love it when they call you for one of your patients. They know you'll stay all night."

He shrugged. "Why not? There's nothing to do at home."

"That's my point, Justin. You need a life beyond the hospital."

Did he? He hadn't considered his daily routine on those terms before because his work had always been his life, even more so after his divorce, but maybe she was right. He couldn't steer Marissa's affections away from Pendleton if he spent every waking moment seeing patients. Then again, if he was a good man, a *gentleman*, he would step aside for Pendleton because he was the one Marissa thought she wanted. However, Justin had never claimed to be a gentleman.

That morning, as he'd showered and shaved, his thoughts from the previous night had coalesced into a semiplan. He couldn't discredit Pendleton because he *had* promised Marissa not to dig up any skeletons in the man's closet, but that didn't mean someone else couldn't do the honors. He had several people he could enlist for such a purpose.

While he was waiting for the right information to surface, he would implement phase two of his plan. Ever since they'd both landed in Hope City, Marissa had been appalled by his spartan living. After his divorce, he'd gotten rid of everything except the barest essentials because he hadn't wanted any reminders of his former life. He'd intended to replace the items, but his long hours of residency had never given him the time. Eventually, he hadn't noticed the lack, either.

Marissa had, though. And she'd hinted, encouraged and sometimes fussed at him to furnish his house as a sign that he'd put his failed marriage behind him. Now he'd use that very situation to draw her attention away from Pendleton.

"Yeah, I've been thinking about that," he said nonchalantly. "I wondered if you could give me a few decorating tips to spruce up my place."

"Decorating tips?" she repeated, her shock apparent.

"Yeah. Haven't you been suggesting a new coat of paint? I need your advice on choosing colors."

She eyed his black trousers and white shirt. "You have been stuck on certain shades," she agreed.

"Which is why I need your help. If you're free, that is."

"You're serious."

"As a heart attack," he replied. "Isn't that what you've been telling me for the last two years? That new paint was the absolute first thing I needed?"

"I didn't think you were listening."

"I was. The question is, are you able to lend your decorating talents to my cause?"

She nodded, her surprise giving way to puzzlement. "Sure, but why now?"

He shrugged. "As you said, time marches on

and change is inevitable. Is Thursday night good for you?"

"Yeah." She bobbed her head, her puzzlement still obvious.

"Travis doesn't have plans?" he pressed.

"He's going out of town this weekend to visit family and then on Monday he's attending a city managers' seminar in Kansas City."

"Fine. It's settled. Thursday night."

Suddenly she shook her head. "I just remembered. Thursday won't work after all. I'm taking Abby to her first childbirth class. Her brother-in-law can't go with her this time."

"No problem. We'll hit the hardware stores on Friday."

"Okay. Mentioning Abby made me remember to tell you that I'm a little concerned about Lonnie."

"What's wrong?"

"His breathing doesn't sound quite right. Everything checks out—no temp, stable respirations, but…"

Marissa had good instincts—part of her magic touch—and whenever she thought something wasn't quite as it should be with a patient, he'd learned to pay attention.

"Okay. I'll have a listen and ask Respiratory Therapy to give him a once-over as well. Has Lucy's culture report come through yet?"

"It printed off this morning," she said, handing over her chart.

"Let me guess," he said before he opened to the correct tab. "Negative for microorganisms."

"Did you expect it to be otherwise?"

He paged through several documents. "Not really. From yesterday's test results I'd ruled out bacterial meningitis, which left viral causes or encephalitis as my diagnosis. And of those two, I'm leaning more to encephalitis because of her altered mental state and the slight droop on one side of her face."

"But you started her on IV antiviral medication right away. Shouldn't we be seeing some sign of improvement by now?"

Marissa's voice held concern, not objective curiosity. No doubt she had expected to see Lucy more responsive that morning than when she had left at the end of yesterday's shift.

"Not necessarily. It may take several days to see any effect."

"But it will work, won't it?"

He shrugged, wishing he could give a guarantee, but he couldn't. "The antiviral agent only works on certain viruses, like herpes simplex or varicella zoster. If one of those two is causing Lucy's problem, then we should see a response soon. If it's another type, like West Nile, then the drug probably won't have much effect."

Her apprehension hadn't disappeared, and rightly so. Viral diseases didn't always react as one hoped or expected—her nursing experience had taught her that. It was simply harder to accept when it involved a loved one, but he'd do what he could to help her remain positive.

"Meanwhile, we'll give her supportive care and wait for her own immune system to fight the battle." He touched her shoulder. "She's a tough bird."

"Even if it is West Nile?"

"Even then. Let's not write her off yet, okay?" Impulsively, he hugged her, and enjoyed how she felt in his one-armed embrace.

Her smile wobbled and she blinked. "I won't."

A high-pitched beep sounded across the hall in room four where his cardiac patient from last night lay. "Time to hang a new IV bag," she said. "While I'm gone, don't forget to write your order for Lonnie's RT."

"Yes, ma'am," he said dutifully. "Now, take care of your beep before it drives us all batty."

Marissa had no sooner left the nurses' station than Kristi appeared. Just the woman he wanted to see. What perfect timing.

"Kristi," he said, pulling her off to one side, out of Marissa's line of sight. "I need a favor."

"If I can. What's up?"

"You've heard about Pendleton and Marissa?"

"Yeah."

"Well?" he demanded. "What do you know about this guy?"

"Not a lot. He's only been in town for a couple of months."

"Does your brother-in-law still work for the city? Has he said anything about his new boss?"

"Actually, Brian is on the maintenance crew and doesn't interact too often with the manager."

"Can you ask him for the latest scuttlebutt?"

She grimaced. "Oh, have mercy. You're doing it again."

"Doing what?"

"Can the innocent act, Doc," she ordered irreverently. "You're hunting for skeletons."

"I'm not," he insisted. "*You* are."

"Gee, thanks. Why am *I* getting involved in your dirty work?"

"Because you're Marissa's friend. Friends look out for each other."

"She won't like this," she warned.

"If people have good things to say, then she'll never know and we'll all be happy."

"I don't want to stick my nose in her business."

"You aren't."

She raised one sardonic eyebrow. "Gathering clandestine information on the man she's interested in is not being an objective bystander."

"Afraid you'll discover that he's not what he's cracked up to be?" If it would only be so easy...

Justin's first impression was that Pendleton was an okay guy, even if he thought a little too highly of himself. If Justin found something to exploit, he would.

"No," she answered warily, "but if I do, then what?"

"We'll tell her."

"Oh, no." She shook her head and waved her hands like a traffic cop signaling someone to stop. "Not me. Forget it. Absolutely not."

"The question is, do you want her to hook up with some guy who'll break her heart because he isn't what he seems? You've been in circulation long enough—you know that what you see isn't always what you get."

She hesitated, then nodded reluctantly. "Okay. I'll call Brian and ask what he knows or can find out."

"Perfect."

"You'd better hope Marissa doesn't catch wind of this," she mumbled darkly.

"How can she? I'm not going to mention it. Are you?"

"Of course not. I don't have a death wish, nor do I intend to lose a friend over this."

He nodded and replied with all seriousness, "Neither do I."

CHAPTER FOUR

"How are you today, Lucy?" Marissa asked on Friday, as she had every morning since her neighbor had been admitted to the ICU.

"It certainly would be nice if a person could actually get more than a few minutes of sleep at a time," the older woman said with a weak smile. "I tell you, there's always someone coming in for something, either to poke me for more blood or to fiddle with my IV." She raised a thin arm with the intravenous tubing taped into place. "Or just to tug on my sheets. And speaking of sheets, tell your laundry people to use a little fabric softener. It's like sleeping on sandpaper."

Marissa smiled. "If you're able to complain about the service, then you're feeling better."

Lucy grimaced as she shifted her hips slightly. "If feeling like a truck dragged me for three blocks is feeling better, then I'd rather skip the 'better' stage and go right to 'normal.'"

Marissa checked the IV pump as well as the array of monitors above her bed. "You will. It's just going to take time."

"I certainly hope I'll get my strength back. I hate being so helpless and shaky." Lucy flexed her age-spotted fingers, but it was plain that her hands shook with a tremor that hadn't diminished. According to the lab result that had just arrived, Lucy's West Nile virus test had been positive. From the few cases Marissa had dealt with before, Lucy would be looking at a long recovery with the potential for lingering side effects.

"I know, but today we're going to try moving you from your bed to the chair and see how you do. And if all goes well, we might see about transferring you to a regular room." While one side of Lucy's face didn't appear to droop as much as it had, a stint of physical therapy would probably be in her immediate future.

"I'd ask about going home but, to be honest, I can't imagine how I'd manage."

"Believe me, we won't kick you out of here until you're ready."

Marissa helped Lucy slip a bathrobe over her hospital gown, then slowly maneuvered her to sit on the edge of the bed. "Don't worry," she said, her grip on the woman's shoulders firm. "I won't let you fall."

Mindful of the IVs and monitor cords, Marissa eased Lucy to her feet. Seeing her dearest friend in such a frail state was somewhat depressing when Lucy had been so filled with vitality before, but at least she had turned the proverbial corner in her recovery. Her temp had dropped to a low-grade fever and her vital signs were strong. After several clearly painful shuffles, Lucy sank onto the padded chair with a heavy sigh.

"Oh, my," she panted. "I hadn't expected to work quite so hard."

"You can have fifteen minutes before it's back to bed. You'll need to rest for a repeat session this afternoon."

"You don't have to tell me twice." Lucy tipped her head back and closed her eyes while Marissa tucked blankets around her. "Did Justin ever decide why I became ill in the first place?"

"He did," she began, but before she could explain, Justin walked into the cubicle. "Speak of the devil," she said instead.

"Did someone say my name?" Justin quipped as he approached the chair.

"Lucy was just asking if you had a diagnosis yet."

"I do," he said with a nod. "The report that I've been waiting for just came through this morning. Your West Nile test was positive."

"West Nile?" Lucy's rheumy eyes narrowed. "What's that?"

"West Nile virus is a virus carried by mosquitoes that have fed on infected birds."

"I've lived a long time, young man, and seen a lot of different diseases and epidemics in my day, but I've never heard of West Nile."

"The virus has only recently come to the Western Hemisphere. It was primarily found in Africa, Asia, Eastern Europe and the Middle East. Considering how people jet from country to country these days, the theory is that the virus 'hitchhiked' a ride to New York and is making its way across the country." He paused. "Had you noticed any dead birds in your yard?"

"A few," she admitted. "I bagged their carcasses and put them in the trash."

"Those birds could have died from the virus, but even if those particular ones didn't, the virus got into our local mosquito population and they passed it on to you."

"I told you that the mosquitoes were terrible this year," Lucy commented. "I had to stop working in my garden during the cool morning hours because of it. With all the rain we had last month, they've been thick."

"When you go home, you'll have to be very careful to stay indoors at dawn, dusk and the early evening when they're at their worst. Don't forget to wear insect repellant and long-sleeved clothing."

"Oh, I will. When did you say I could go home?"

He exchanged a smile with Marissa. "I didn't. First we have to move you out of ICU to a regular room. If you manage being out of bed today, we'll give you a change of scenery tomorrow.

Then maybe a week or two should be enough to get you back on your feet."

"Another week?" The wrinkles in Lucy's forehead deepened. "Oh, but my garden. My flowers."

Marissa patted her shoulder. "I've watered every other day, just like you did."

"Thank you, dear, but the weeds will have completely taken over by the time I get home."

"You won't be able to weed," Justin cautioned. "At least not at first. You need physical therapy to regain your strength, and even then you'll tire easily. I'm afraid that we're looking at a long recovery period at home."

Lucy's bony shoulders stiffened. "Weeds wait for no man," she said.

"I can't promise we'll do as good a job as you do," Marissa jumped in, "but Justin and I will do what we can this weekend." If she was going to become his interior decorator, then he could lend a hand at pulling a few weeds.

"Are you sure?"

Marissa smiled. She'd walk through a blizzard to help Lucy and told her so.

Lucy's eyes brightened with merriment. "I do hope that won't be necessary, my dear. I appreciate your help though." She glanced at Justin. "Yours, too."

"My pleasure. Just don't snicker when you see me on Monday, all bent over and stiff as a board."

Lucy giggled. "You young people just don't know how to handle physical labor."

Justin leaned over and spoke in a loud whisper. "Now you know why I went into medicine, but don't tell anyone."

This time, Lucy laughed aloud. "Oh, go on with you."

"Do you mind if I borrow Marissa for a minute?" he asked her.

Lucy waved her gnarled hand. "Take your time. I'm not looking forward to the trek back to bed anyway."

Outside the cubicle, Justin steered Marissa toward the nurses' station. "Be prepared—Galen Stafford is admitting one of his patients to your unit as we speak. Another suspected West Nile case."

The news sent a shiver down her spine. Before she could comment, he continued.

"There's also a nine-year-old boy in the ER who's worse—he's slipping in and out of a coma."

Immediately, she mentally ran through their pediatric supplies. "Are you admitting him here?"

"George Martin, the pediatrician, is airlifting him to a children's hospital."

"We're going to get bombarded, aren't we?"

"It's very possible. The pathologist announced at our staff meeting this morning that he's seeing a dramatic increase in positive West Nile test results. Granted, not all of the patients are as sick as the ones you're seeing now, but it's a definite cause for concern."

"So what do we do?"

"I'm trying to reach our county health department. The sooner we start alerting people to the dangers and instruct them on proper precautions, the better. Meanwhile, are we still on for tonight?"

She smiled. "Yeah. I'll meet you at your house at seven."

"You'll have to backtrack because the hardware store is past your house."

"That's okay. I want to walk through your place first and get some ideas."

"I thought you had the colors already in mind? Or so you've always said."

"I do, but I want to look at your floor plan with a fresh eye."

"Okay."

He sounded far too cooperative. Suspicious, she asked, "Are you feeling well?"

"Yeah, I'm fine. Why?"

"I know you don't like change."

"It isn't that I don't like change," he corrected. "I just don't need it for its own sake. Besides, we're only talking a coat of paint. As long as you don't ask me to move the dishes in my kitchen cabinets around, I'm fine."

"Dishes?" She covered her mouth in mock horror. "You actually have dishes?"

"Yes, Ms. Smarty-Pants, I do."

"Then I'll see you at seven."

"If I'm not there—" he began.

"I know where you keep your spare key."

As he strode away, she watched him leave, wondering if aliens had somehow taken over Justin's body. She shouldn't look a gift horse in the mouth—she'd been begging him for the last two years to make his house a place he'd *want* to go home to, and he'd fought her tooth and toenail. Now, out of the blue, he was ready for a makeover.

Granted, painted walls didn't constitute a makeover in the true sense of the word, but they were a change. And for a man who was happy with a bland, off-white appearance throughout his house, agreeing to different colors was a significant move. Although she'd badgered him often, he'd withstood her subtle hints as well as her not-so-subtle ones. Now, almost overnight, his position had shifted and without any prompting on her part. Curiosity made her wonder at his sudden about-face, but if she pressed him for his reasons, he might stop the project before it got started. Some things were better left unanalyzed.

Satisfied with her decision, she returned to Lonnie Newland's cubicle.

"I thought you were going to sleep in this morning at home," she chided, as soon as she saw Abby seated in the chair beside the bed. "Especially after you stayed so late last night after the birthing class ended."

"I was," she admitted as she straightened in the

chair. "But Junior…" she rubbed her tummy in a circular motion "…woke up early. I thought I may as well start my day, too."

"Are you getting enough rest?" Marissa demanded gently, seeing the dark smudges under her eyes.

"My day consists of sitting at home and sitting here, then back home again. Add a few walks around the hospital and my house, and then I'm sitting again. I'd say that's plenty of rest."

Perhaps she was getting enough physical rest, but emotionally she wasn't. What the poor woman needed was for her husband to respond, but each passing day made hope dwindle.

"Thanks for going with me last night," Abby said again. "I really appreciate it."

"Anytime. I'm always available—" Before she could finish her sentence, the distinctive sound of a plugged airway caught her attention. "Why don't you step outside for a few minutes while I take care of this?" she told Abby.

Weariness crossed the young woman's face as she nodded, then left the room.

Marissa suctioned Lonnie's airway and, once

finished, shifted his arm and leg positions to prevent bed sores. It never failed to amaze her how quickly a healthy body deteriorated as the weeks marched on. As active as he'd been, his once muscular extremities were now pale and skinny. "Squeeze my hand, Lonnie," she said, watching for the slightest movement that might indicate he was still inside his weak frame.

Nothing.

She patted his hand and laid it back down. If they were able to kick his pneumonia, Abby would have to face the next step of placing him back in a facility that specialized in the caring for and rehabilitation of brain-injured patients.

A practiced glance at his body showed no outward change from her last visit, so she concentrated on the monitors that recorded those details invisible to the naked eye. Dissatisfied by his oxygen saturation level, she made a mental note to call Respiratory Therapy. And as she was already in the room, she ran through her usual physical exam to look for any signs of complications. Her trained fingers felt pulses while she listened to his heart, lungs and abdomen for sounds that might translate into one of any number of diagnoses. Pleased by her lack of abnormal findings, she checked the nasogastric tube that delivered the vitamins and minerals to keep his body alive, and ran through the rest of her tasks.

She charted her observations, then met Abby in the hallway.

"All done?" Abby asked brightly, or as bright as a seven-month pregnant lady under severe stress could be.

"For now. Can we talk a minute before you go in?"

Marissa hated taking people to the family room because it was the place where, more often than not, a staff member delivered bad news. While her conversation wasn't going to cover topics that hadn't already been brought to Abby's attention, it was the only private place available on their unit.

"I know Dr. St. James has already discussed this with you," Marissa began as soon as she closed the door, "but we wondered if you'd changed your mind about a 'do not resuscitate' order."

"No." Abby shook her head and paced a few steps. "I can't. Not yet. Signing it would be like

I'm giving up." She rubbed her belly. "And I can't. Not yet." Her eyes held a plea. "Not as long as there's a chance he could wake up and see our baby."

Marissa now privately thought it was highly unlikely, but she could only echo what Justin had told her before. "He's not responding to our treatment for his pneumonia as well as we'd like. His last EEG doesn't show much activity."

Abby squared her shoulders. "I can't give up hope. Maybe tomorrow, but not today. You understand, don't you?"

God help her, but she did. Marissa couldn't imagine what it must feel like to see one's soul mate become so helpless and dependent on others for even the simple act of breathing. But Abby was due to deliver their first child in a matter of weeks. The stress of changing the status quo, making a decision that she wasn't emotionally ready to make, would only be added stress at a time when Abby didn't need it.

"I understand." She hugged Abby. "Go on in and take a load off your feet. RT will stop by to collect a blood gas shortly."

"Thanks."

As Marissa retraced her steps toward the patient cubicles to help Kristi with the other potential West Nile victim, she wished that she could stroll down to Central Supply and requisition a magic lamp with a genie. Even if she were only granted one wish, she couldn't imagine spending it on anyone more deserving than Lonnie Newland.

"What do you think?"

Marissa paused in her final survey of Justin's living room as she heard his step in the entryway and the clang of car keys landing on the kitchen table. Unwilling to let him see how affected she was by the things she'd seen, she swallowed the strange lump in her throat and managed a smile as she turned to face him.

"Well," she began, searching for a diplomatic answer, "it's what I'd expected." She'd arrived to an empty house some thirty minutes earlier and had sauntered through each room, trying to understand how such a vital and virile man like Justin could have lost so much interest in his personal surroundings since his divorce. At first, she'd wanted to weep at how Justin had chosen to live with only the barest necessities, as if enduring penance for the loss of his marriage and the wife of his dreams, but by the time she'd completed her circuit, she'd started to focus on the possibilities instead, much like an artist stared at a blank canvas and saw the final result.

"That bad, eh?"

His crestfallen expression made her all the more determined to be diplomatic. This was, after all, the place where he'd chosen to live, and even if it was a far cry from anything she'd consider welcoming, pointing out every flaw would only put him on the defensive. It had taken him a long time to agree to fresh paint, and she certainly didn't want him to back out before she'd accomplished that much. If she played her cards right, she might also convince him to add new curtains and a few more pieces of furniture. And if she was *really* lucky, she just might talk him into new carpeting as well. But any journey began with a single step, and she intended to make sure this one started without a hitch.

"Well," she began again, "your place is certainly sterile-looking." The living room boasted a leopard-spotted sofa, a black leather recliner and a battered rectangular coffee table that held a haphazard assortment of medical journals and electric train magazines. A lone mountain lake landscape hung on a wall.

"Sterile?" He looked as puzzled as he sounded.

"As in plain, austere," she explained.

Understanding filled his eyes. "I prefer the "no-clutter" look."

"I can tell." She wondered if he truly preferred no-frills living or if he'd simply gotten used to doing without. His divorce had left him with little more than the clothes on his back and an empty bank account, but he'd claimed those terms had been preferable to paying his ex-wife alimony for the next ten years. Whatever his reason, she intended to convince him that his house didn't have to look as bare as a monk's cell.

"Fresh paint will definitely be an improvement," she said, turning slowly as she imagined how the room *could* look, "but you really should consider a few other changes, too."

His eyes narrowed. "Knocking down walls is out of the question."

"I'm giving decorating tips, not remodeling advice," she countered. "I'm simply saying that sometimes one project leads to another. For example, when I replaced the shower in my bathroom, the new tile made my sink look old-fashioned. After I tore that out, then the flooring didn't look right. The same thing might happen here."

"We're only painting the walls," he reminded her.

"True," she agreed, "but speaking from experience, you should prepare yourself to replace those window shades and curtains."

"Is there anything else I should *prepare* myself to replace?" he asked wryly, as if he suspected that she wouldn't be satisfied with only a new coat of paint.

"Maybe one or two other things, but I'll let you know when they come up," she answered airily.

"Whatever ideas are percolating in your head, don't get carried away," he warned. "I don't want the house to look like it belongs in a magazine. I only want it to be comfortable, a place where I can throw my socks on the floor and leave my newspapers without bringing down the interior design police."

"Somehow, I can't see you living with clothes tossed haphazardly in every room." A mental picture of his underwear trailing across the house sent an anticipatory shiver down her spine. Briefs or boxers? she wondered, but after a quick perusal of his snug jeans, she decided upon briefs. He'd look as good as he had when she'd seen him wearing swim trunks some ten years ago, probably better.

He shrugged. "I'm turning over a new leaf."

"Really?"

"Really."

"Fat chance," she disagreed. "Some things are just too ingrained. In you, neatness is one of them."

"I can be a slob as easily as the next guy." He grinned. "You'll see."

"Let's not go that far," she said, "but I get your point. You want a place that has a homey, lived-in feel."

He nodded for emphasis. "Exactly. It shouldn't be too hard to create, should it?"

"Not if you're giving me carte blanche."

He chuckled. "Not a chance, Mari."

"I'd work within a budget," she volunteered.

"My budget only allows for paint."

She snapped her fingers. She hadn't expected him to allow her to perform a complete makeover, but it hadn't hurt to try. "Shucks."

"But I'm willing to thoughtfully consider any other suggestions."

All hope wasn't lost. "Well." She sighed dramatically. "That's better than nothing."

"I *am* the person living here."

"Then I don't suppose you'll approve my idea of white lilies stenciled on lilac walls."

He grimaced. "Smart woman. Try again."

"Okay. How about this?" She grew serious. "You need warmth in here, so I'm thinking beige, not creamy or off-white but a shade darker that will contrast nicely with the oak woodwork."

His focus seemed to soften as he imagined the mental picture she'd painted. "Not bad."

"For the kitchen, let's go for bright and sunny." At his frown, she modified her plan before he could completely veto it.

"I'm not talking taxicab-yellow bright and

sunny. Think creamy yellow, with a cheery wall-paper border to bring in more color."

"No flowers," he ordered.

"None?"

"None," he said firmly.

"What's wrong with—?"

"Chandra papered every room of our apart-ment with floral prints. I felt like I was living in a sixteenth-century boudoir."

"Okay, then. No flowers," she dutifully echoed, happy that he'd allowed yellow instead of his favorite, albeit boring, off-white. "Now, in your bedroom—"

"What's wrong with my bedroom?"

"I'll show you." She marched inside the room and threw her arms wide. "Look at this."

He surveyed the room. "Yeah, so?"

"You have a clip-on light clamped to your bedframe instead of a table lamp."

"I like to read in bed," he defended himself. "Besides, I don't have a table *for* a lamp."

"That's my point. You also have a black towel hanging at the window. A *terrycloth towel*, Justin."

"I know it's not fancy, but the curtain fell apart and a pillowcase didn't block out enough sun."

"A pillowcase?" She rolled her eyes. "What's wrong with buying a new curtain?"

He shrugged. "No time to shop. Anyway, the towel works fine. Better than the curtain that had been there, in fact."

She pinched the bridge of her nose and forced herself to speak normally, instead of yelping in horror. "That may be, but if we're going to spruce up this room, the towel has to go."

"Okay. We'll paint and buy a curtain."

"And maybe a picture or two for the walls."

He winced. "I come in here to sleep, not study artwork."

"Pictures break up the monotony. Prison cells have more character than your room, Justin."

He grinned. "Been in a lot of them, have you?"

"You know what I mean," she said tartly. "The only things that reflect *you* in this whole house are the family photos you've hung in the hallway and the pharmaceutical coffee mugs in the kitchen. I can't believe your mother and sisters didn't give your house a face-lift when they stayed with you after the accident."

It seemed somewhat of an understatement to refer to the plane crash as simply an accident, but after all these months, the event still packed enough punch to give Marissa nightmares. She'd never forget the heart-wrenching fear or the knee-weakening relief she'd experienced during those hours of his rescue.

"Not for lack of trying," he said wryly.

"How did you stop them? I've met your mother and she can be rather forceful."

"They were given a choice. If they brought one unauthorized thing into the house, then they had to leave." His grin was sheepish. "I was a bear afterward, so they didn't cross me at the time."

"And now?"

"I visit them at their places so their sensibilities aren't outraged when they come here."

"How thoughtful."

"Ain't I, though?" He snickered.

"As I was saying about the bedroom—"

"You won't stop hounding me until I slap something besides paint on the walls, will you?"

"One painting, Justin. That's all I'm asking."

He frowned, then his shoulders slumped with resignation. "Okay, but only one."

Her smile felt as if it stretched from ear to ear. It probably did because she'd made a promising start to his home makeover. Little did he know that she had an entire scenic grouping in mind, but that revelation would wait for another time. "Just remember," she warned, "a bedroom should be a relaxing place that draws you at the end of a long, hard day."

"Relaxing, eh?" He stroked his chin as he wiggled his eyebrows. "I can think of other things that I'd rather do in here than relax."

Unbidden, her gaze fell upon the rumpled bedsheets and a pillow that still held the faint indentation of his head. Considering how tangled the bedding was, if she didn't know him as well as she did, she might have wondered if he'd entertained an overnight guest.

An anticipatory shiver shot down her spine, leaving a surge of heat in its wake. With any other man, she might have thought he was flirting with her, but with Justin? No, he was couldn't deny the one hard truth that Justin had already pointed out.

If she loved someone enough to sleep with him, she wouldn't notice the decor at all.

simply being his usual teasing self, just as he'd been in college. How silly to read more into his comments or to get all hot and bothered by her imagination.

Determined to deny her reaction—which she shouldn't be having at all if Travis was the man she hoped to marry someday—she went on the offensive.

"Then you're definitely going to strike out if you bring a girl in here," she countered. "The ambience does *not* set the tone for a romantic interlude."

His jaw squared. "I wouldn't bring a woman in here if she was going to pay more attention to my furniture than to me," he grumbled.

"Of course not, but this is *the* most private room of the house and it's where she'll see the real Justin St. James. Not just the side of him that he wants her to see, but every little thing. No games, no pretenses, no secrets."

"I'll say," he said dryly as his mouth twitched with undisguised humor.

"Oh, be serious," she chided. "This room, of all rooms, has to reflect *you*—your personality, your innermost self."

"If you want reflections, I'll install a mirror over the bed."

The image he'd created, with her fantasies writing her into the scene as well, nearly took her breath away. Certain he was only trying to get her proverbial goat because friends didn't flirt with each other, she scolded him with the proper amount of affront in her voice. "Would you stop joking for a minute and listen?"

"Okay, okay." His teasing smile disappeared. "What do you suggest?"

"Dark, masculine colors," she decided as she pivoted slowly. "Maroon, navy blue, moss green. A solid cherrywood dresser and nightstand. Maybe even a four-poster bed…."

"Hmm A four-poster bed?" He idly stroked his chin. "Interesting. I wonder if a scalpel is strong enough to carve notches in wood."

She paused as she crossed her arms and tapped one foot. Once again, his irreverence reminded her of their late-night college library conversations. "If you're going to make inappropriate remarks…"

"I won't. Please, go on."

"The point is, if you ever invite a woman share your space, the room needs to project t image that she's the only one who's ever bee invited into your purely masculine domain. Ros petals and candles aren't necessary, but sh needs to feel that she connects with you on mor than a purely physical level. That *she's* the one who's finally entered your most private domain, that *she* and not some other woman will be the one who'll make the evening memorable to you. That's what I would—"

She stopped herself before she could say "want." Yes, that was what she would want if she were ever to be invited into Justin's bedroom for more than decorating tips.

Her unfinished sentence, uttered with such passion and a dreamy wistfulness, echoed in the silence. Suddenly afraid that she'd revealed more about her innermost thoughts than she should have, she pointedly checked her wristwatch.

"Look at the time!" she exclaimed. "If we don't get to the store soon, it will close before we can pick out paint chips."

Yet, as he accompanied her to his car, she

CHAPTER FIVE

MARISSA'S conversational slip-up hadn't escaped Justin's notice. Nor had the way she'd rattled off her ideas for the living room as if she'd been afraid to let him get a word in edgewise. Sidetracking him she was, all the way to the hardware store, but rather than put her on the spot by asking questions that she clearly didn't want to answer, he simply smiled and nodded at appropriate intervals. Little did she know that while he physically sat in the driver's seat of his car, he mentally remained at his house.

He'd heard the longing note in her voice as she'd described what *she* wanted in a man's bedroom, which only led him to believe one of two things—either she'd never seen Pendleton's *private domain* as she'd called it, or, if she had, he hadn't delivered her specific fantasy.

Which only made him suspect that if she could create the atmosphere she wanted in *his* bedroom in comparison, then it might cause her to look at Pendleton through less awestruck eyes.

To that end, no matter what she suggested—paintings, drapes, a four-poster bed—he would approve. Not at first, of course, because he didn't want to raise her suspicions if he suddenly or enthusiastically agreed to every idea. He'd allow her to convince him, because her gorgeous smile, when she thought she'd won an argument, was worth the small drain on his checking account.

But what if she really loved *this guy?*

She couldn't, he decided. She'd only known Pendleton a few weeks. Love didn't sprout overnight, at least not the abiding sort that lasted through thick and thin and was worth fighting for when times got tough. Although…if by some fluke of nature she loved Travis wholeheartedly after only a short time, did he have any right to interfere, even under the guise of trying to save her grief? Was that why his friends had kept silent about Chandra? Would he have listened, or would their warnings have only driven a wedge between them?

"What's wrong with this color?" Marissa asked.

"What?"

"You were frowning. What don't you like about this shade of yellow?"

He glanced at the paint chip. "It's fine. I was just thinking of something else. A patient," he improvised rapidly.

"Oh." She turned back to her paint chips and his attention switched back to his thoughts.

Okay, he told himself. Maybe his friends hadn't felt that it was their place to interfere, but he'd known Marissa for a very long time. What sort of friend would he be if he didn't warn her of potential danger? If she loved the guy, nothing he did would change the way she felt. If she didn't, then it would be far better if she discovered that now rather than later.

Aren't you being devious...and selfish?

Maybe he was. He would certainly lose a lot if Pendleton and Marissa had a long-term relationship, but the point was, he was doing this for Marissa's own good. If Travis wasn't the right man for her—and he wasn't—then she needed to know that before he broke her heart.

* * *

By mid-afternoon on Sunday, Marissa almost regretted her decision to tackle so much of Justin's home improvement project at once. Painting three rooms and a hallway hadn't seemed like a monumental task at first, but after working until midnight on Friday and from sunup to sundown on Saturday, she had revised her opinion. Her arms and shoulders ached from wielding screwdrivers, paintbrushes and caulking guns, and her legs quivered like gelatin after climbing up and down ladders for hours.

Although Justin didn't complain, she'd caught him flexing his muscles from time to time, too. She'd also noticed the way he'd favored his weaker right hand and arm during their lunch break, and she knew she had to call a halt for his sake as much as her own. She would have to be creative about it, though, because if he suspected that she was catering to his weakness, he'd balk like a Missouri mule.

"I don't know about you, but parts of me that I didn't know I had are aching," she remarked as she rubbed the back of her neck. "Would you be offended if we call it a day after we finish the living room?"

He laid the paint roller in the tray and flexed his fingers. "I thought you wanted to do all of the painting this weekend."

"I did, but I'm beat. Even if we stop now, we've still made good progress. It shouldn't take more than an evening or two to slap the second coat on your bedroom and kitchen. Then, next weekend, we can add the borders."

He dipped his roller in the paint tray. "Planning to soak in the tub tonight?"

"I wish," she said fervently, "but Lucy's weeds are waiting for me and Toby desperately needs another bath."

At the mention of his name, Toby lifted his head from his place on the sheet-covered sofa. His normally dark beard appeared gray and his fur sported several yellow and green splotches.

"He does look the worse for wear. Silly mutt," he said fondly, as he shifted the roller from his right hand to his left and flexed his fingers.

"Nosy mutt," she corrected, casting a benevolent glance at her pet. "Paint-stained paws aside, he could use a good run in Lucy's backyard. And *I* could use some fresh air."

"You've convinced me. We'll wrap this up and call it a day."

A few minutes later, Marissa stepped back to survey their efforts with a critical eye. Satisfied, she smiled. "Nice job, St. James."

Justin paused to swipe his forehead with his forearm. "Good, because it's going to be a very long time before I do this again," he grumbled as he dipped his roller in the paint pan again.

"If that's the case, maybe we should repaint the other two bedrooms while we're going to all the trouble." Toby uttered a single woof. "Even Toby agrees."

"Not a chance. He's just pushing us to finish so he can play outside."

"Could be," she admitted. Then, because Justin's arm movements seemed stiff, she volunteered, "I can work on that wall if you like."

"I'll do it," he said firmly as he transferred the roller to his less dominant left hand and attacked the wall with more enthusiasm than skill, which explained why paint spatters covered him from head to toe and why Toby had taken up residence on the sofa in the middle of the room.

"I'm impressed. You're becoming quite ambidextrous."

He shot her a glare. "I wouldn't go that far, but at least with painting I get by. Why don't you rinse out the brushes while I take care of this last section?"

"Good idea. But before I go, you missed a spot."

"Impossible. I'm using enough paint to cover a city block."

"That might be, but that spot…" she pointed "…needs another swipe."

He peered at it. "Looks fine to me."

"Trust me. It needs another swipe."

"All right, all right. Slavedriver," he mumbled.

"And don't you forget it." Smiling broadly at him, she sailed into the kitchen with her brushes.

Humming a happy tune as she rinsed the bristles under the kitchen spigot, she couldn't deny the sense of accomplishment resting within her. Her vision for his house was slowly taking shape. Before long, Justin's place would be as homey and welcoming as hers.

He probably didn't realize it—there wasn't any way that he could—but it was important for her to do this for him. If things worked out between her and Travis, she didn't want Justin to lose the haven he'd found in her little house. She wanted his own home to be a place where he'd want to relax and unwind, to entertain friends and create happy memories, not merely be a place to crash when he had no place else to go. Whether he realized it or not, this would be her final gift to him.

The thought should have left her with that warm, fuzzy feeling of contentment, but it didn't. Instead, an ache shot through her chest—a bittersweet ache of things lost.

Not lost, she told herself firmly, falling back into her old habit of using logic to counteract her secret desires. One couldn't lose what one had never had. Justin saw her only as a friend, nothing more, and bemoaning that he never had was counterproductive. Just as she had found someone special in her life, Justin would someday do the same, and she would do well to remember that.

In the meantime, she had a dog who needed to stretch his legs and weeds calling her name.

She shut off the water and dried her hands on a paper towel. "How are you coming in there?" she called out.

A crash was her reply, followed by a hearty bark and an even louder human expletive. Marissa rushed to the doorway and held back a giggle.

The overturned paint can told the tale. A puddle was growing in an ever-widening circle underneath it while Justin stood nearby, liberally covered in tan paint, with a few blotches on his face for good measure. Rivers of tan ran down the walls to pool on the woodwork and dropcloths. The sheets protecting the furniture were also lavishly sprinkled, with some areas saturated enough for paint to drip onto the floor. Toby stood on the sofa, his tail in the air and his eyes wide, looking as surprised as Justin.

"What happened?" she asked, afraid he'd tripped over something she'd left behind.

"I dropped the damned can," he ground out.

His disgust with himself was painfully obvious. "Accidents happen," she said lightly. Then, because he'd hate it if she made a fuss, she didn't. "I'll help you clean up the mess."

"I made it, I'll clean it up," he snapped. "Go back to whatever you were doing."

"I was almost finished anyway," she began.

"I'll take care of it."

The finality in his voice told her that he wouldn't appreciate her assistance. Reluctantly, she nodded. "Okay, but I'll be back in a few minutes."

He righted the can and nodded. Marissa hated leaving him alone to silently stew about his short-comings, as she knew he would. Ever since the accident, he'd taken his perceived imperfections completely to heart when as far as she was concerned, they weren't worth the mental anguish. Today's mishap could have happened to anyone, including someone without a hand weakness. Yet she had no choice but to honor his request.

She left without a word and returned to the kitchen where she blotted the brushes dry. When she couldn't stand the silence emanating from the other room any longer, she returned.

Justin didn't acknowledge her presence because he was too busy staring at the huge stain on the carpeting that the overlapping plastic sheets hadn't been able to prevent. Wordlessly, she carried out the offending paint bucket, as well as the roller and tray. As soon as those items were stowed away for short-term storage, she found Justin sitting next to Toby on the sofa, his face drawn.

Marissa snapped her fingers and Toby jumped to the floor so she could take his place. As soon as she sat down, she reached for Justin's right hand and began her gentle massage.

His muscles felt stiff under her fingers and she silently berated herself for being responsible. "I should have taken this project more slowly," she apologized softly, "but you know me. I don't do anything in half-measures."

A half-smile tugged at his mouth. "It isn't your fault. I didn't do anything that I didn't want to do."

She wasn't willing to let herself off the hook. "I pushed too hard."

"Believe it or not," he said wryly, "I know my limitations." This time a faint but distinct smile appeared. "Even if I don't always act like it. God, that feels good." He leaned back and closed his eyes.

She massaged his wrist and forearm. "I'm

glad." She continued to rub at the tension knots, enjoying the feel of his skin beneath her fingers before she moved down to his hand again.

"I'm going to beat this."

She wasn't certain if he'd commented for his own benefit or hers. While the orthopedist had agreed that Justin had progressed far better than he'd initially hoped, any further gains couldn't be predicted. She didn't want Justin to harbor false hope, but she didn't want him to give up, either.

"I know," she said softly, easing up on the pressure she'd been applying.

"I hate this."

"I know," she repeated. Justin had never been the sort to pander to his own weaknesses, although he didn't judge those who did. He simply held himself to a higher standard. A guy thing, she'd always assumed. Unfortunately, while that attitude might work for minor aches and pains and sprains, some things fell outside the realm of possibility.

"You could have died," she continued practically. "A weak wrist seems a small thing in comparison to losing your life."

"Yes, but—"

"While you're waiting and working toward a full recovery, don't undo all the progress you've already made. I won't think any less of you if you have to take a break every now and then. Neither will anyone else."

At his nod, she added, "If you look at the bright side, a couple of good things came out of this."

His eyes popped open. "Oh?"

She concentrated her healing touch on his palm. "I now have an official gofer."

He chuckled. "Says who?"

"Says me. Someone has to 'gofer' things like soda and snacks and more paint."

"More paint?"

She giggled at his horrified expression. "Relax. I was only giving an example. We shouldn't need any more paint, unless you decide to spill a full can instead of a nearly empty one."

"Not if I can help it," he said fervently. "So what's the other good thing?"

"From the size of that stain, I foresee new carpeting in your future."

He sighed. "I was afraid of that."

"The sofa, too."

He groaned. "Not my sofa. It may be the ugliest thing known to man, but it's comfy."

"Only to you," she corrected. "The fabric is rough and scratchy and feels like my grandpa's Second World War green army blanket."

"Maybe we could just rearrange the room."

The hope in his voice made her smile as she shook her head. "If we set it so the splotchy side faces the wall, we'll ruin the traffic flow. Feng shui and all that."

"Who cares about feng shui?"

"You'd also have to move the television out of the corner where the cable hook-up is," she pointed out.

"Why?"

"Because you can't see the screen if the sofa is over there. Not a good idea."

"No problem. I'll run a long cable."

"People will trip over the cord."

"Then I'll ask the cable company—"

She cut him off. "Buy a new sofa, Justin. It will be so much easier all round."

"Don't sound so happy."

"I'm not." She grinned. "Not much, anyway."

"If I didn't know better, I'd think you'd planned this whole thing."

"Caught me red-handed." She inched her way up his arm once again. "How's that?"

"Perfect. Better than perfect. If you ever become a massage therapist, schedule me for a weekly appointment. You can work absolute magic."

Somehow she didn't think she'd survive rubbing her hands all over his body. Her professionalism would only stretch so far.

"Thanks for the vote of confidence, but I'll leave that field to someone else." She reluctantly drew her hands off his arm. "There. You're good as new."

"Think so?"

She smiled. "Other than the paint blobs here and here." She touched his right cheekbone and felt the stubble on his face. Impulsively, she trailed her finger down to his mouth.

His utterly kissable mouth.

"I'll take care of those later." He grabbed her hand. "Thanks, Mari. For everything."

Before she could guess at his next move, he tugged until she leaned forward and rested her palm against his chest. His lips brushed against hers in a featherlight caress before the light pressure gave way to a deepening, demanding kiss that required a response.

Without thinking of the consequences—she'd dreamed of this moment for years and, as with all forbidden fruit, she couldn't resist the taste— she gave it willingly, surrendering to the moment, completely in awe of the power that this innocent, unplanned action had generated. His kiss—no, *The Kiss*—was everything she'd ever imagined. It reminded her of the electrical charge in the air right before a thunderstorm, when anticipation of the coming fury sent one's heart into overdrive and heightened every sense.

And she was enjoying it far, far too much.

But, then, why shouldn't she? She was twenty-nine, almost thirty, and she'd never experienced a kiss with such power before. It wasn't as if she hadn't kissed anyone—she'd kissed enough frogs in her lifetime to know the routine—but none of those guys had made her toes curl like Justin did.

Not even Travis.

What was she doing? she thought wildly. She

shouldn't feel this way—no, she *couldn't* feel this way because it wasn't right with Travis waiting in the wings.

Yet it *did* feel right. An urge to sink against him rolled over her, as well as a desperate desire for more.

Before she could wrap her mind around the concept of what she wanted "more" to be, Toby's crisp bark broke the spell.

She pulled away, hoping Justin hadn't noticed just how close she'd been to losing control, chagrined that it had even happened and even more grateful to Toby for standing guard over her conscience.

Clenching her fist to stifle the residual feel of his heartbeat against her palm, she avoided Justin's gaze to glance at Toby. The Cairn terrier stood before her, his black eyes piercing and his head cocked in a way that seemed to reflect both puzzlement and curiosity.

I'm just as confused as you are, Tobe, she thought. However, from the way Toby jumped into her lap, his confusion clearly hadn't lasted as long as hers.

Justin chuckled as he laid his long, capable fingers on Toby's head and began scratching behind his ears. "You just wanted a piece of this action, too, didn't you, buddy?"

A sound came from Toby's throat, as if he agreed.

A piece of the action. As far as she was concerned, there had been no action. This had only been a simple kiss from a man she'd known for years, a simple kiss of thanks for working the kinks out of his muscles. That's all it had been. That's all she would let herself imagine because she'd moved on with her life long ago.

Defusing the situation—before he asked questions, she couldn't answer—became her top priority. Later, she'd think about the implications but for now she needed a witty, lighthearted remark to smother the sparks in the air. To say anything serious would only give the incident more importance than it deserved. Better to treat "The Kiss" as inconsequential, because it was. After all, the man had far more experience in that department than she did—one more area in which he excelled.

"Wow, Justin," she remarked, striving for a

carefree tone as she avoided his gaze, "with kisses like that, I'm surprised you've only been married once. Remind me to toss your name in the hat for the hospital's next bachelor date auction. Once word gets out, you'll bring in a fortune for the fundraiser."

"Don't even think it," he threatened.

"In any case," she continued primly, as if he hadn't spoken, "you're welcome." She grabbed Toby off the sofa and jumped to her feet. "Things are under control here, so I'll run home and scrub Toby down or he'll be spotted until his next haircut."

He rose, too. "I'm coming, too. You'll need help with Lucy's chores and you volunteered me to help out in her garden, remember?"

"You don't have to bother," she said, striding to the door with a wiggling Toby under her arm. Eager to leave, she didn't want to waste time chasing her dog through Justin's house. Toby was far too comfortable here, probably because he had so many more things to explore, not to mention the joy of being a pet vacuum for all the stray crumbs that slipped past Justin's housecleaning efforts. "Weeding won't be good for your hand. We wouldn't want to undo all the work I just did."

"I may not pull weeds, but I take my job as a gofer seriously. Thanks again for all your hard work, Marissa," he said as they reached the front entrance.

She had a sudden urge to release Toby and hug Justin instead, but succumbing to the notion after his ground-moving kiss would be sheer folly. Justin wasn't interested in long-term relationships with anyone, much less her, while she, on the other hand, had a bright future with Travis. She didn't have any business cultivating any more dreams or fantasies about the man in front of her.

Unfortunately, those facts and admonitions barely softened her yearning. Stunned by her completely illogical and impossible thoughts, she gripped Toby like a protective talisman until he whimpered in protest.

"Sorry, Tobe," she whispered, before she spoke to Justin in her normal voice. "You're welcome. Again."

As she dashed to her car, she told herself not

to read more into The Kiss than she should. The man had been completely unaffected by the incident—he hadn't sounded hoarse or surprised or shown any reaction whatsoever. But why should he? He'd only been thanking her as a friend who'd performed a favor, and she would do well to remember that.

What in the world had just gone on? Justin asked himself as soon as Marissa had dashed to her car. His heart was still pumping as if he'd set a new record for the mile and the feel of her soft skin was indelibly imprinted on his.

After she'd finished working out the kinks in his hand and wrist and he'd gotten over his pity party, his natural impulses had taken over. Where those had come from he didn't know, but he couldn't have asked for a louder wake-up call.

He'd only intended to give her a thank-you peck, but it had led to him pulling her into his arms in a most natural embrace, which she hadn't resisted. What was even more startling was how once he'd tasted her mouth and breathed in her scent, he'd wanted to carry her off to the bedroom that her decorator sensibilities disdained and turn her fantasy into reality.

He couldn't remember the last time he'd been this sexually frustrated, and it hit him hard. Obviously, his subconscious had seen Marissa as a desirable woman long before his conscious mind had. After a kiss that had only whetted his appetite for more, seeing her in the same platonic light as before would be like trying to stop the wind. Completely impossible.

Situations that he couldn't explain up to now started to make sense—the reason Pendleton's interest in Marissa had unsettled him, why Lucy's comment about them being a couple hadn't sent him recoiling in horror, why it had hurt to know that Marissa hadn't considered him to be her type. Why he was jealous of Travis, and why he was determined to push the other man out of her life.

They were all signs of his feelings for her that went beyond friendship, but he hadn't recognized them.

Or maybe he simply hadn't wanted to.

For a man who'd believed that love wasn't

for him, it was a shock to realize he still felt those emotions after all this time. Or was he suffering from a simple case of lust? A repeat of the early days in his relationship with Chandra, when he'd been thinking with his hormones instead of his heart?

No, this situation wasn't quite the same. He hadn't had the history with Chandra that he did with Marissa. He hadn't known her as well as he knew himself, which was an apt description of his relationship with Mari. The question was, *was* he ready to love again?

Maybe, he thought, if he was certain he wasn't responding to the heat of the moment.

And if he was, what was he going to do next? More importantly, what did he *want* to do next?

He was still too poleaxed to know, but from the way Marissa hadn't been able to rush out of his house fast enough, she had clearly been as shocked by the magic of their kiss as he had. She had responded just as eagerly and in the end had appeared just as confused.

Lucy had mentioned something about building on the foundation they'd already laid. *Could* they build a relationship stronger than friendship? A relationship that would last, a relationship that he might be willing to label as love at some point in the future?

He had no choice but to try. If he failed, so be it, but he'd fail for sure if he gave up without a fight. Considering how he'd experienced his epiphany before Pendleton actually slid a ring on Marissa's finger rather than afterwards, when it would have been too late, maybe Fate had a hand in what came next.

In the meantime, he had petunias to weed and a dog to bathe.

On Monday morning, he met Kristi as she walked into the nurses' station. "Where's Marissa?" he asked as he glanced furtively down the hallway.

Kristi sat in front of a computer terminal and began entering her notes. "She went to the lab to pick up a unit of blood. She won't be back for at least ten minutes."

"Good," he said, straddling a chair next to her. "What have you found out about Pendleton?"

Kristi sighed. "I don't like this sneaking around business at all. It's going to get us both into trouble."

"Objection noted. Go on."

She cast a long-suffering glance at him before she sighed. "Here's what I've learned so far. Most people say he's a decent sort, although he has a tendency to act a little lofty. He works hard and he works late, which is quite unlike the last city manager we had. He's a fanatic about watching the bottom line, which isn't necessarily a bad thing."

"Everyone likes him?"

"Most are still reserving judgement. Several have mentioned that he's good at office politics. They've almost all said that he won't last long here in Hope—he's more interested in bigger and better things than our little community. So far, no one has any huge grievances against him."

That wasn't what Justin wanted to hear. "Surely he has some flaw."

She shrugged. "Sorry, but if he does, no one's saying what it is. The only real complaint I heard was how he's determined to trim the budget of each department by twenty percent. Again, that isn't unusual—making do with less seems to be the way of life these days."

"Yes, but trimming the budget doesn't win friends."

"Some of his cuts haven't been popular," she admitted, "but it's only to be expected. No one wants to give up the equipment or services that they're used to having. My cousin, Harold, says that he's slashed the maintenance department's budget to ribbons."

"How so?"

"Less money for herbicides and other chemicals. Which means they'll either spray less or switch to lesser quality products. In any case, it's something that the public probably won't care about. No one frets over dandelions or chickweed in a city park. And don't forget how good it will look on his résumé if he can say that he singlehandedly balanced the city's budget."

So much for Justin's hopes of finding something to exploit.

"No other gossip or dirt swept under the rug?"

"Nothing that anyone's talking about." She paused. "What's next?"

He rose. "I'll let you know. Just keep your eyes and ears to the ground."

"If you ruin this for her, she'll never speak to you again," Kristi warned. "She doesn't want or need a big brother."

He patted her shoulder as he rose. "Not to worry. I have everything under control."

"Under control? Really." She didn't sound convinced.

"Really."

Kristi leaned back in her chair and crossed her arms. "If you successfully run Travis off, she'll have a hole in her life that *you* created."

"I know."

"Well? What are you going to do about it?"

Suddenly wary, he asked, "What do you mean?"

"Men," she muttered as she rolled her eyes. "I mean, are you going to keep pretending you're only friends and keep chasing off all of the eligible males until you stop having cold feet, or are you finally going to step up to the plate yourself?"

Wary, he asked, "What do you mean? We *are* friends."

"Oh, come on," she said with exasperation. "I know married couples who don't see each other as often as you two do."

"We're friends," he repeated, while wondering if he sounded as uncertain as he felt. "We have a lot in common."

"Sure you do."

"What's that supposed to mean?"

She swiveled her chair to face him. "I'll be honest. Your relationship with Marissa has always puzzled me. You're friends, but you're not."

He narrowed his eyes. "I don't follow you."

"You're friends, but you act like you're more than that. I understand what you're trying to do with Travis, but you're being a lot more overprotective than a normal 'friend.'"

"I am not."

She crossed her arms. "Then name one other 'friend' you've tried to save from a bad relationship."

He opened his mouth, then closed it with a snap.

"See? If you ask me, you aren't sure if you want her, but you certainly don't want anyone else to have her either. Deny it all you want, but from where I'm sitting, you have a roaring case of cold feet."

She was right, but old habits—and painful memories—died hard.

Kristi leaned forward in her chair. "I don't know anything about your ex-wife or your marriage, but Marissa is a different person. She deserves more from you than crumbs."

He winced as her comment struck home. He *had* given Marissa crumbs of himself, but that had been all he'd had to give. That, however, didn't excuse him for denying her something better from someone else. Realizing it only made him feel even more selfish and shallow.

Again, what was his next step? Because it was his to take.

"Thanks for holding back and sparing my feelings," he said facetiously.

"Sorry." Kristi sounded unrepentant. "Just think about what I said. If the shoe fits…"

As if he could do anything else but think! In the meantime, he had a house to redecorate.

* * *

Marissa had never been so glad for Monday morning to arrive. While nothing more had been said about her ideas for Justin's bedroom—thank goodness—the memories of their kiss had surfaced with astonishing regularity.

That would all disappear, she told herself, as soon as she spoke with Travis. Because he'd planned to return tomorrow night, she would make a point to touch base with him some time the next day. Maybe then she'd stop obsessing over something so minor as a kiss between friends and put her focus on the *real* relationship in her life.

In spite of the weekend's few unsettling moments, in retrospect she couldn't complain too loudly. They'd accomplished a lot on Justin's house, weeded Lucy's garden adequately, even if they had accidentally pulled a few petunias along with the crabgrass and henbit, and all the paint had washed out of Toby's fur.

Unfortunately, those same few days hadn't turned out as well for Lonnie Newland.

"His pneumonia isn't getting better, is it?"

Abby asked with a worried frown as she rubbed her rounded abdomen.

"He's not responding to the antibiotics as quickly as we'd like," Marissa said diplomatically. "Respiratory Therapy is going to collect another sputum sample for culture. Lonnie may have picked up a new bug and if so, we'll need to either change his antibiotic or add another one."

Abby stroked her husband's thin, pale arm while Marissa checked his monitors and the urine in his drainage bag. The poor man didn't need a urinary tract infection to fight along with everything else.

"And his seizures?" Abby asked softly.

Marissa had learned during the shift report that Lonnie had started having seizures on a daily basis and his heart rate had become irregular. Again, his anticonvulsants and digoxin dosage had been modified at midnight and everyone hoped these changes would do the trick. Still, considering his overall condition, those signs weren't good.

"We'll control them as best as we can," she murmured.

Abby nodded, more in acknowledgment than agreement. "He opened his eyes yesterday," she said. "He smiled at me and squeezed my hand before he went into a seizure. God, how I've missed seeing his smile."

Her voice quavered. Marissa didn't have the heart to explain about involuntary reflexes, but she didn't have to.

"I know what you're thinking," Abby continued. "Those were just reflexes or muscle spasms, or whatever, but for those few seconds it was like he was still at home. You know what I mean?"

Marissa nodded. "Yes, I do."

For a few minutes Abby didn't speak and only the familiar bleep of the equipment punctuated the silence. "Dr. St. James asked me again about signing a 'do not resuscitate' order." She paused, her throat working as she stared down at her husband with a bleak expression on her face.

"It's a tough decision," Marissa agreed. "You have a lot of issues to consider."

Abby nodded slowly. "I know I should let him go, but I can't. Not until after the baby's born. After we found out I was pregnant, he brought home something different every day." Her hazel eyes took on a far-away gleam. "First it was a baseball mitt, then it was a doll. He went back and forth between planning for a boy or a girl." She smiled. "He said he wanted to be prepared either way."

"So do I look for boy things or girl things?" Marissa teased.

"I can't say for sure." Abby grinned. "But something tells me it's a boy." In the next breath, she rubbed her tummy and winced as she bent forward. "Wow, that was kind of strong for being a Braxton-Hicks."

Marissa helped her to the bedside chair. "Are you sure that's all it is? Maybe you need to call your obstetrician."

"I've had these off and on all week and Dr. Jennings didn't seem concerned. I'm sure if I sit for a few minutes, they'll ease."

A distant ding caught Marissa's attention. Although she hated to leave Abby, she had other patients to tend. "If they don't," Marissa advised her, "push the call button and I'll be back before you can say, 'Let's have a baby.'"

"I will."

But before Marissa reached the doorway, Abby groaned and doubled over. Baby Newland clearly wanted to arrive.

"Let me call your doctor," she said.

Abby shook her head. "No. Not yet. But if you'd call Eric to ask if he could drive me home…?"

Eric was Abby's birthing coach as well as Lonnie's brother, and as such his phone number had been posted in the nurses' station. "Absolutely. I'll let you know just as soon as I reach him."

Luckily, Eric answered on the first ring. "I'll be there within fifteen minutes," he promised.

Relieved, Marissa disconnected the call. Thank goodness Abby wouldn't go through labor by herself.

And yet Marissa wondered if having someone other than the man Abby loved at her side would make her feel less alone. Somehow, she doubted it.

CHAPTER SIX

JUSTIN had been trying to think of a way to see if their friendship could become something more, but he hadn't come up with any brilliant ideas. The only thing he could do was what he always did—spend time with her—and hope that the right plan would pop into his head at the right time.

He caught up with Marissa just as he finished his ICU rounds. "Are you interested in checking out the new barbecue place?"

"Well…" She hesitated.

"I'm buying," he coaxed.

Marissa smiled at him. "What's the occasion?"

"An early thank-you for your redecorating talents."

"In that case, yes, I'll go. When?"

"How about tonight?"

"We were going to look at carpet samples," she reminded him.

"First we shop, then we eat. I'll pick you up at six thirty."

She'd hardly had time to agree before his pager summoned him to the medical unit. "What's up?" he asked the puzzled-looking young nurse, whose nursing pin sparkled with newness and whose name tag read "Ellie."

"It's Mr. Dalton in twelve," she reported. "We've followed your protocol to the letter all weekend, but his finger-stick glucose is all over the place. It's either really high—over three hundred—or very low. Do we need to change his dosage or switch to another type of insulin?"

Justin frowned as he reviewed the numbers. "He's already on a combination of long- and short-acting insulin. This is the same dosage that we used to stabilize him in ICU." Kyle had been diagnosed with diabetes a week earlier when he'd arrived by ambulance, unconscious because his blood glucose had been over six hundred.

"Someone hasn't changed his diet by accident, have they?" he asked.

She shook her head vehemently. "I've double-checked with the dietician. I've also asked the aides who've been delivering his meal trays. They all insist he's gotten the proper tray."

"Good thinking." Mistakes sometimes happened when a busy nurses' aide misread the placard.

"Then what's the problem?"

"If I were to guess, I'd say our patient isn't cooperating as fully as he should," he said wryly. "I'd better have a little chat with him."

However, the minute Jared walked into the room, the cause for his patient's erratic glucose was blatantly obvious.

Sixty-two-year-old Kyle Dalton was sitting in bed with a doughnut in his hand and powdered sugar covering his upper lip.

"Well," Justin began, glad that he'd found the cause so quickly and irritated by his patient's decision to go against his medical advice, "this explains a lot about your bloodwork. I'm one hundred percent positive that the cafeteria didn't send that up with your breakfast."

Kyle dropped the remnant of doughnut back into the white bakery bag and brushed the sugar off his mouth while looking suitably chagrined. "Sorry, Doc," he said. "But your cooks just don't send up enough to eat. I'm as hungry after a meal as I was before. That just can't be right for a fellow as active as I am. And what they do send tastes downright awful. Runny eggs, stone-cold sausage links, chicken noodle soup that's basically water with a few noodles and a piece of chicken dragged through it for flavor just ain't what I call real food."

While Kyle's manual labor job as a construction foreman gave him plenty of exercise, he definitely needed to trim away at least fifty excess pounds.

Justin turned to his wife. A mousy woman in comparison to her husband, it was easy to guess that she had spent her marriage bowing to her spouse's wishes. "I assume that you've been bringing the doughnuts?"

She nodded sheepishly as she avoided his gaze. "I had to," she said. "I got tired of him whining and complaining about being hungry. And he's really cut down since he's been here," she hastened to assure him. "A doughnut or a candy bar here and there is all."

Justin drew a deep breath and fought for calm. For the most part, his patients followed his professional advice in order to either become or stay healthy. Unfortunately, there were a few who thought medicine would provide a magic bullet to unhealthy lifestyle choices, and Kyle was one of them.

"We may not have a gourmet chef on staff, but you absolutely can't eat those," he addressed Kyle sternly. "Unless you don't care about developing irreversible complications that develop because of uncontrolled glucose levels."

"I've always had a sweet tooth," Kyle said defensively. "Can't you just increase my insulin to counteract the sugar?"

"That isn't the way this works," Justin said firmly. "Diabetes requires a lifestyle change, so indulging your sweet tooth with pastries…" he motioned to the bakery bag "…has to stop. If you aren't going to follow my advice, then I may as well discharge you now. But I promise you'll be back in the ER before long, probably in a coma that is potentially irreversible.

"And if you think that having a machine breathe

for you and being little more than a vegetable is easier than cutting the doughnuts out of your diet and losing weight, think again. I'll be happy to wheel you upstairs to visit a man who *is* comatose and has no hope of recovery, so you can see what I'm talking about. If you choose to go that route after you see him, I won't stand in your way."

Of course, Lonnie Newland's reason for being in a coma had nothing to do with diabetes, but the end result was still the same.

Indecision appeared on Kyle's face. "You're just trying to scare me," he began.

"Yes, I am. If the possibility of a coma won't scare you into following orders, then maybe the idea of living with the effects of a stroke or being blind will. Then there's the poor circulation and infections that could force us to amputate one or both legs."

He raised an eyebrow. "Do those sound like better prospects? Because I can guarantee you'll eventually experience one or all of those situations if you continue what you're doing."

Kyle's face blanched. "You're serious, aren't you?"

"Dead serious. I've seen a lot of people who manage their diabetes perfectly and live a normal life. I've also seen people who ignore the potential side effects and complications, and they pay the price. The choice is entirely yours."

A pregnant pause followed.

"So what'll it be?" Justin pressed. "My way or your way?"

"I'll follow my diet," Kyle reluctantly admitted.

"No extra food?"

Kyle winced as he avoided Justin's gaze. "None."

He turned to Kyle's wife. "And you won't cave in and bring things he can't eat?"

"I won't," she promised.

"I'm going to hold you both to your word," he told them sternly. "If not, you may as well start looking for another physician. I can't help you if you won't meet me halfway."

"Oh, that won't be necessary, Doctor," Mrs. Dalton said, casting a frown in her husband's direction, at the same time squaring her thin shoulders. "He'll be a model patient."

Kyle nodded, his face resigned, while Mrs. Dalton seemed to stand a few inches taller. If

Kyle cheated again, it wouldn't be with his wife's blessing.

The rest of his day went swiftly and smoothly, and Justin found himself glancing at the clock and counting the hours until he could be with Marissa again. It was strange, really. He'd never done that before, or at least he'd never noticed. Although this evening wasn't technically a date, he found himself wishing that it were. Who knew where it might lead?

In the end, it led exactly where he'd expected. First to the carpet store, then the restaurant. As they waited for the waitress to deliver their food, he realized how easy it was to be in Marissa's company. There were no awkward moments of silence when the conversation lagged, no worries about putting one's best foot forward, no mincing words to avoid potentially saying the wrong thing. They knew each other too well for that.

Which only reminded him that he hadn't known Chandra half as well. Oh, he'd known the superficial stuff, but with Marissa, their knowledge of each other went deeper than her favorite color or gemstone. Maybe the two of them had a chance after all….

Marissa scanned the homey decor of the restaurant with its red checkered tablecloths, lit candles, comic pictures of fat little chefs on the walls, and napkins large enough to be towels. The atmosphere at Buck's Barbecue was as boisterous as a Fourth of July picnic, and every now and again, someone would slip money into the jukebox to hear their favorite country and western song.

"This is quite a place," she said above the din.

"It is. I hear the food is terrific."

Marissa eyed the steaming platter of ribs that a waiter had carried to a nearby table. "There's certainly plenty of it. I predict we're going to need a carry-out box."

"At least one," he agreed. "But with all those bones, Toby will be in doggy heaven for a couple of days."

"If he gets them at all," she remarked.

"You're not going to share?"

"Probably not," she admitted. "I don't want

him to break off a piece and choke on it and I definitely don't want him dragging a bone slathered in barbecue sauce through my house."

He grinned. "You don't want to buy new carpeting, too?"

She laughed. "After seeing the prices, I can't afford it. But of those we saw, which sample did you like most? And don't say the cheapest one."

"How did you guess?"

She shook her head. "You'll never change, will you?"

"Oh, I don't know," he said lightly. "I might surprise you."

While they discussed the merits of the different samples they'd chosen, Marissa noticed how all the patrons appeared to be couples. One couple in particular caught her eye when she saw the two of them holding hands across the table. Suddenly, she wished that she and Justin weren't just two friends sharing an evening meal but a couple on a bona fide date.

Immediately she scolded herself for her wish. It was so unlike her to let her thoughts continually stray in the wrong direction. Travis was coming home, Justin wouldn't need her decorating tips after a few more days, and then her life would finally get back on an even keel. It was so odd that after all their years of easy camaraderie, something had changed between them. Oh, they still talked and joked, but the underlying atmosphere was different, as if the air had suddenly become electrified.

All because of one little kiss.

Logically, she knew she'd handled herself well. She'd treated the incident lightly, as if it had meant nothing. He hadn't mentioned it since, which only suggested that he'd dismissed it from his mind far more easily than she had. She would do well to follow his lead.

Yet when he leaned across the table with his napkin to dab at her mouth as soon as she'd finished her meal, something flashed in his eyes for a split second.

"Barbecue sauce," he explained.

She wiped her mouth again, with her own napkin. "Thanks." Yet, it didn't take much imagination to picture him kissing the same spot.

Sweet mercy, but she was definitely in trouble!

* * *

If Justin had harbored any doubts about there being enough sparks between them to take their friendship to a new level, they'd disappeared after last night's dinner. He'd heard her little intake of breath when he'd dabbed at the sauce at the corner of her mouth, seen how her gaze had landed on his lips and how her eyes had softened with her smile. He would never have noticed those things if he hadn't been alert, which only made him wonder how many other signs he'd missed.

In any case, Marissa wasn't as immune to him as she pretended.

He would have liked to mull over the situation and figure out where he would go from here, but after Jared Tremaine, Hope's ER Director, caught him on his way out of the hospital the next morning, the opportunity disappeared.

"Have a minute?" Jared asked.

"Barely. What's up?"

"You missed the medical staff meeting this morning."

He snapped his fingers. "Darn. I forgot."

"The main topic of discussion was West Nile. The local news has picked up on the number of cases reported in the county and wants to interview a doctor to discuss symptoms, treatment, preventative measures, etcetera."

"Good idea. Who's the poor schmuck, er, lucky person, who gets to go on the record?"

"You."

He groaned. "Me? Why me?"

"Because you're the closest thing we have to an infectious disease specialist."

"Norm Allen likes to go in front of the camera. Let him have the honors."

"He's eighty if he's a day and only sees a handful of patients in between his fishing trips. I'm not sure he knows any more about West Nile than the reporter does."

"What about—?"

Jared shook his head. "No arguments. You're it. We voted and the consensus was unanimous."

"But I wasn't there to defend myself," he protested.

Jared grinned. "Let this be a lesson to you. He who doesn't attend gets volunteered. It happens every time. Honestly, St. James, you should know that by now." He shook his head in mock sympathy.

"I don't suppose I could claim being too busy as an excuse."

"Not a chance." Jared clapped him on the back. "Look at it this way. You know all the details off the top of your head while the rest of us would have to do our homework. Plus, you've treated the most severe of the cases we've seen in the area. Never let it be said that we didn't pick the best man for the job."

"Gee, thanks."

"Your interview, by the way, is at five. I purposely scheduled it at the end of the day so it wouldn't interfere with your office hours."

"I'm thrilled by your thoughtfulness," Justin said dryly.

"You also might want to touch base with Virginia at the County Health Office. I understand she's going to participate, too."

Justin sighed. "Anything else?"

"Not at the moment," Jared mentioned cheerfully. "If I think of something, though, I'll call you. Catch you later."

Justin marched toward his car, wishing someone else had been chosen to stand in the limelight. While the article would be timely, considering the number of positive West Nile tests the medical community had encountered, he'd rather spend his time with Marissa, redecorating his house. Not to mention how he had to somehow convince Marissa that Pendleton wasn't the man he was cracked up to be.

And yet maybe this interview wasn't such a bad thing after all. Comparing notes with Virginia just might give him the ammunition he needed.

All at once, he created his own list of questions, but he intended to get his answers long before five o'clock.

And he did.

Now he only had to think of a tactful way to break the news to Marissa.

"I'd like to see Travis Pendleton," Marissa informed the City Hall secretary shortly after six-thirty that same evening. She'd been on her way home after work when she'd decided to spring an unannounced visit on Travis to welcome him back, in person, from his trip. Although they'd spoken on the phone every night he'd been gone, she felt like an eager teenager now that he'd come home.

"He's still on the phone, but go on back and have a seat." The twenty-something blonde wearing a crisp navy suit gave her an inquiring look before she waved her in the direction of his office. "He won't be much longer, I'm sure."

"Thanks."

A minute later she hesitated outside his doorway. Although his secretary had given her permission to enter, she hated to simply barge inside. Rather than interrupt, she waited...and watched.

He may have spent the entire day at the office, immersed in whatever tasks were required to manage the city, but she couldn't tell it from his appearance. Not a hair was out of place and although he'd abandoned his suit coat, his tie was firmly in place and his white shirt unwrinkled. Cool, calm, and collected came to mind while she, on the other hand, was definitely not looking her best.

She tucked a few wispy strands of hair that had

slipped out of her ponytail behind her ears, wishing she'd stopped to powder her nose. Her tracksuit, although of wrinkle-free cotton polyester, had spent the day wadded up in her locker since she'd changed into her scrubs at the hospital early that morning. Perhaps she should have gone home and slipped into something classier, like her best pair of black dress slacks and a silk blouse, to welcome Travis home after his trip.

While she debated the merits of slipping away, sight unseen, he saw her, smiled broadly, then waved her in. "Have a seat," he whispered with his hand over the receiver. "I'll be through in a minute."

She sank into the plush side chair, pleased that he hadn't minded her impulsive visit. Determined not to listen to his one-sided conversation, she mentally compared the samples of kitchen wallpaper that Justin had liked and tried to decide which of the three would fit him best. Before she knew it, she was comparing the man himself to the one in front of her.

By this time of day, Justin would look rumpled. He would have discarded the jacket and rolled up his sleeves, appearing like a man who'd been physically active, not like one who'd hardly moved a muscle. Because he considered ties a nuisance and an infection hazard, he would have gone without. Some of his colleagues might consider a tie part of a physician's uniform, but not Justin. Even while working, he dressed for comfort, not style.

You're not being fair, she scolded herself. Travis worked just as hard at his job. The difference was that Travis spent his day in a very public position that demanded a proper, businesslike appearance. His career might not be as physically demanding as a doctor's, but he wasn't a slouch. He visited the health club religiously every evening and played basketball on the weekends.

So? her little voice asked. *Would Travis have helped her weed Lucy's garden this last weekend? Helped her scrub Toby clean?* Probably not, she admitted. In the short time she'd known him, he'd made it plain that he believed in getting the best man for the job. Which meant that a professional would have been called to look after Lucy's garden. As for Toby, an appointment with a dog groomer would have been in order.

Would he have listened to her opinions about decorating his apartment or, better yet, would he have even asked *for her opinion?*

From what she knew of Travis's personality, lifestyle and aspirations, he would have hired an interior decorator rather than attempt a do-it-yourself project, but she wouldn't fault him for that, either. In his position, entertaining was a given and image was extremely important.

And Justin's image wasn't?

Of course it was, she answered herself, but Justin knew that she enjoyed being creative. The subject hadn't ever surfaced with Travis—they didn't have the same long history that she and Justin had—so she couldn't subtract points from his column because he didn't know her well enough yet.

Points? Good heavens, what was she doing? The two men were apples and oranges, and even if they weren't her potential for a future with Travis was far greater and more rewarding than her future with Justin.

Travis's voice broke into her thoughts. "We've cut some of our expenditure in the maintenance department," he said. "All of our departments were affected. Not only the groundskeeping section.

"The chemicals we use are standard products, used by a lot of communities across the country for weed and pest control. The product we're using is more cost-effective.

"We are concerned about the mosquito problem. Our maintenance staff have been targeting those areas of town where we have drainage problems." He paused. "We don't currently have plans to spray residential areas. Hope is a fairly large community and we simply can't cover every square inch at the present time. I understand those communities with massive spraying programs in place have also had cases of West Nile. Those with the disease have my sympathies and I wish them all a speedy recovery."

He cut off the call, leaned back in his chair and smiled broadly at her. "Well, well, what a surprise. What brings you here?" he asked.

Marissa had a hard time shifting thought gears.

"I, um, was on my way home and thought I'd stop by and ask how your trip went."

"It was great. I made a number of good contacts at the seminars I attended and have a lot of new ideas to implement. With luck, I'll put Hope on the map," he crowed.

"Progress is good," she pointed out, suddenly aware that his large personal goals included big dreams for the town, as well. She didn't disagree with his ambitions, but she didn't want to sacrifice the essence of Hope on the altar of city development.

All at once his motives seemed suspect, and it became easy to put two and two together. He seemed far more interested in building his résumé than in actually building the town into a place where the residents enjoyed living, both for the short and long term.

"Hope is already on the map," she said. "It may be small by some standards, but it is growing."

"On a limited scale," he agreed. "But its potential is far greater. We need to capitalize on our strengths and use them to our advantage to bring people into town. For example, not only do we have some of the best lakeview scenery, but our medical community is top-notch. We need to promote those things."

She seized the opening. "Speaking of medicine, I couldn't help but overhear your discussion about mosquitoes."

"Unfortunately, our *Hope Daily News* reporter thinks the city is singlehandedly responsible for the local West Nile cases," he said wryly.

Because of Lucy, this subject was near and dear to her heart, so she wanted to sound him out. "Oh? What makes him think that?"

"Our budget cuts are no secret. Unfortunately, some of them aren't popular. Mosquito control is one that fell by the wayside."

"You're not serious, are you? You've eliminated the program?"

"It isn't as horrifying as you think. We're using a more cost-effective chemical now, and only spray in those parts of town where our crews have found standing water. Because we're focusing on the five or six problem sites, we've cut our usage by two-thirds. With prices being what they are, we can't afford to treat the entire town."

"We used to." She remembered how notices would appear in the newspaper, telling people to close their windows on the nights when fogging took place.

"Yes, and the city hasn't met its budget for the past five years," he reminded her. "I was hired to bring the finances into line, and I'm doing that."

"But what about all the people who use the city parks?" she persisted. "The kids who play baseball and tennis? Not to mention everyone who mows their grass or gardens or simply spends time outdoors?"

"People have to assume responsibility for themselves. I can't help it if they choose not to wear mosquito repellant or the proper clothing when they're outdoors."

"This is summertime," she pointed out. "Children aren't going to stop, change into long pants and long-sleeved shirts before they go out to play."

"There are chemicals available for home lawn use, not to mention all of the other mosquito elimination gadgets on the market. People can buy the level of protection they want or need, rather than expect the city to foot the bill."

"That's a rather cold attitude, don't you think?" she asked, irritated by his attitude. "Especially with this being a public health issue?"

He moved to sit on the edge of his desk. "Now, Marissa, you surely don't believe that the government should micromanage people's lives."

"This isn't micromanagement," she insisted. "This is about people's health and quality of life. My neighbor contracted West Nile in spite of taking every precaution she could. People are doing their part to limit their risks, but the city has to do its part, too."

"She has my sympathies, but when we were reviewing our expenditures, I had to draw the line somewhere. We just don't have the finances. I'm sorry."

"But can't you cut other areas?"

"Look, Marissa. I appreciate your concern, but do I tell you how to do your job?"

"No," she said slowly.

"Then don't tell me how to do mine."

Hearing the rebuke in his voice, she rose. How

had an innocent welcome-back visit turned into a debate? "I understand what you're trying to do, but I won't apologize for wanting to protect people's health."

As she turned toward the door, he grabbed her hand. "I don't expect you to," he said. "Your compassion is what makes you so very special."

His compliment should have made her feel better but, oddly enough, it didn't. Instead, his flattery reminded her of the time when Kristi's two-year-old nephew had wanted an expensive toy truck in the store and she had diverted his attention with a gumdrop. Marissa, on the other hand, refused to be distracted as easily.

"Then, as a favor to me, will you look into this further? See what you can do?" she pressed.

He fell silent for several seconds, his gaze intent. "I don't suppose you'll rest until I tell the maintenance crews to include all the city parks."

His offer was a less-than-ideal compromise, but it was better than nothing. "It's a start," she said.

"It's the best I can do."

Although a "take it or leave it" comment went unsaid, it was implied. "Thank you." She offered a bright smile, which seemed a fair enough reward. "A lot of people will appreciate your change of heart."

"Good. As we've ironed out that issue, I'd better get back to work." He motioned to his paper-laden desk. "As you can see, I have a few more things to take care of before I can call it a day."

"Of course. I didn't mean to interrupt." She headed for the door, then stopped, once again the peacemaker. "It's good to have you back, Travis."

"Thanks," he said. "It's good to *be* back."

Marissa walked through the now-vacated building, glad that their relationship was back on friendly terms. And yet, deep down inside, something still didn't set quite right. She'd always been so impressed by his goals, career plans, and impeccable manners that she hadn't seen his lack of concern for the people he was supposed to serve. She couldn't imagine Justin being willing to save a few dollars at the expense of his patients' welfare.

Don't make unfair comparisons, she chided herself. Being tired, she was simply overreacting to the situation. So she didn't see eye to eye with his choices about where to save money. There were probably a lot of other, equally important programs that hadn't got the proverbial axe.

But did they involve public health? her little voice asked.

It was hard to say and it certainly wasn't her place to decide, she told herself firmly. The point was, every couple had differences of opinion. It didn't mean they weren't right for each other. Besides, he'd listened to her arguments, then compromised, hadn't he? What more could she want?

Once she'd laid her doubts to rest, she realized that she hadn't confirmed their dinner date for the following evening. It seemed ridiculous to phone him later when she was in the building, so she quickly retraced her steps to Travis's office as she planned her menu.

She'd grill this time. After dining out for the past several days, he'd probably welcome a bit of home cooking. Rib-eye steaks, twice-baked potatoes, a Caesar salad and her special chocolate caramel cheesecake for dessert would make the perfect meal. Satisfied by her ideas, she poked her head into his office.

Her words died in her throat as soon as she saw the two people inside.

She didn't mind seeing his secretary—the woman had every right to be there. After all, there had to be times when they would need to work together on a particular project.

What Marissa *did* mind, however, was seeing that same secretary wrapped in Travis's enthusiastic embrace, with her form-fitting blue skirt exposing long legs and her opened shirt revealing a lacy black bra.

And Travis—the rat!—was kissing her with enough passion to light up Main Street on Christmas Eve.

CHAPTER SEVEN

MARISSA froze, too stunned to do more than gape like a landed fish at the two of them. Surely she was dreaming. Travis had been too attentive, too polite, too *sincere* toward her for this to be happening.

And yet it was.

Undeniably.

She must have a made a sound, because the two broke apart and glanced at her with matching looks of surprise and embarrassment. Within seconds, the young woman recovered enough to adjust her clothing while Travis sheepishly straightened his tie.

"Marissa," he said weakly. "I thought you'd gone."

"Obviously," she replied calmly. Later, when she was alone and the shock had worn off, she'd experience the full gamut of emotions. At that moment, she felt numb.

"I'd only come back to confirm our dinner date," she continued, "but under the circumstances, I'd say it isn't necessary." How ironic for her to have considered their relationship as exclusive, while he clearly had not.

What a fool she'd been!

Anger began to build, but she refused to act on it. Somehow it seemed important to treat the situation lightly as a matter of pride. Letting him suspect that her feelings had run deeper than they plainly should have would only make him laugh at her naiveté.

She stepped forward and extended her hand. "We haven't been introduced. I'm Marissa Benson."

He filled the breach. "This is Tanya Hathaway. She's my secretary."

"Administrative Assistant," Tanya corrected as she limply shook Marissa's hand. "Nice to meet you."

"We were working late," he began.

"Oh, I can see that," Marissa said airily. How blind did he think she was? "Budget issues, no doubt. Anyway, as I can see how busy you both are, and as what I was going to ask you is no longer important, I'll leave you two to carry on."

This time she found her way to the entrance in record time, but before she could open the door Travis reached around her and held it closed.

"I can explain," he began.

"I'm sure you can," she said through gritted teeth, wanting to escape before she did something foolish, like burst into noisy tears.

After she beaned him with her purse, of course.

"Tanya and I've had an on-again, off-again relationship," he began. "I didn't think we could ever work through our differences, so—"

"From the looks of things in your office…" she motioned over her shoulder "…I'd say you did. How long have you two been back together?"

"Since yesterday. Our reconciliation came as somewhat of a surprise," he admitted.

I'll bet. She swallowed her words because, no matter what, she would weather this with grace. He would never know just how badly her own imagination, wants and desires had run amok. Thank goodness only two people knew—Kristi and Justin. And if Travis hadn't been so flamboy-ant with his flowers, only Kristi would have known.

"Anyway, when I met you, I thought I was ready for an entirely new relationship. But…" He shrugged.

"You weren't," she finished. "I understand." She didn't. Not really. "But I wish you'd told me about her. You should have."

Once again, he didn't defend himself.

She held her keys with a death grip and took a deep breath. It seemed pointless to cast blame at this stage or belabor the facts. Their relationship was over before it had even had a chance to develop. She knew that now.

"I wish you both well."

"Thanks. I'm sorry for any misunderstandings."

She was, too. "I only have one question. Why all the flowers? Were you hedging your bets with me or simply trying to make Tanya jealous?"

He opened his mouth, then closed it as if unsure of what to say.

That small action spoke volumes.

"On second thought," she added, with a small

smile that cost her, "don't answer. I'd rather keep the fantasy."

"I'm sorry, Marissa."

If she heard his apology one more time, she was going to strangle him with his tie. As if "I'm sorry" would be enough to salve the hurt of lost dreams.

"We had a lot going for us," he continued. "If Tanya hadn't been in the picture…"

Unable to choke out a reply and definitely unable to feel grateful over her runner-up status, she tugged on the door and hurried to her car. Tears burned behind her eyes and threatened to spill down her face but she held them at bay by sheer force of will.

Life would go on, she told herself. Losing Travis wasn't the end of the world.

Then why did she feel like it was?

Justin had been trying to reach Marissa all evening. After his interview with Rick Miller, a two-car collision on the highway leading into town, two chest-pain cases, a broken hip and the usual assortment of minor emergencies had sent their small ER staff scrambling for additional coverage. Being the man on call, he'd come in to assist, which meant that he hadn't been able to help Marissa with the second coat of paint as planned.

He'd left a message on her home answering machine as well as her cellphone's voice mail, asking her to return his call, but she hadn't. Now, at nine o'clock, with the crises under control, he still hadn't heard from her. No matter. He'd drop by her place later in order to reschedule.

Her house, however, was dark, suggesting that she wasn't at home, so he checked out her usual haunts. No one, including Kristi, had seen her.

"You've got bigger problems," Kristi told him. "I found out a few minutes ago that our illustrious city manager has a girlfriend on the side."

"What?"

She nodded grimly. "An assistant or something in his office."

"That sorry piece of—" He cut himself off as he ran his hands through his hair.

"Yeah, well, I said something a little stronger when I found out. The question is, does Mari know and if she doesn't, how are we going to tell her?"

He shook his head. This news would devastate

Marissa. Not only that, but if he told her, she'd probably shoot the messenger. Provided she believed him, of course.

What to do?

"Before I can do anything, I have to find her." He'd deal with the other issue later.

She had to go home sometime and so, with that thought in mind, he returned to her place. Unfortunately, her property appeared as deserted as it had thirty minutes earlier. No one answered the door or turned on the lights in response to his knock.

Worry set in, but short of asking the police department to issue an all-points bulletin to find her, all he could do was to leave more messages on her phone.

As he turned away to return to his car, he heard a muffled bark and scratching at the door. Toby was never allowed to run loose if Marissa was away from home, yet he clearly had free rein. Which meant that she had to be at home, too.

A bad feeling settled in his gut. Something was wrong—he knew it as well as he knew his own name. The question was, what?

Without giving his actions a second thought, he flipped through his set of keys until he found the spare that Marissa had given him for an emergency. This qualified, he decided, as he let himself inside.

Toby greeted him with a happy woof.

"What's up buddy?" he asked as he bent to scratch the dog's ears. "Where's Marissa?"

The dog cocked his head, stared intently as if to ask him to follow then calmly trotted away in the direction of the living room.

Justin followed. Other than the sound of toenails clicking on the wood floor, the house was silent. The situation was puzzling, but the Cairn's easygoing manner was somewhat reassuring.

"Saving on electricity, Mari?" he teased as he walked past the kitchen and clicked on the light. "I can float you a loan if you can't pay your bill this month."

He found her in the family room, in the dark, watching television with the volume set at a few notches above a whisper. "Here you are," he said, reaching to activate the table lamp's switch.

She must have expected him to do just that, because she said, "Don't," her voice husky.

His concern over her physical health might have faded, but something was definitely wrong. The television's glow guided his steps to the sofa where she sat with Toby curled in her lap. Even with such limited visibility, he could make out her red nose and the dark circles under her eyes. She'd obviously taken a shower because her hair was wet and she was wearing an oversize bed-shirt that read BOYS ARE STUPID.

A box of tissues rested beside her while the coffee table held a pile of wadded Kleenex, a bottle of Chardonnay, a single long-stemmed wineglass and a half-empty bowl of popcorn.

"Drowning your sorrows or celebrating?" he asked.

"I haven't decided yet."

"Oh. Mind if I have a seat?"

"Actually, you could just go on home. I'm not in the mood for company."

"Then it's a good thing I'm not considered company." He plonked down next to her. Wondering what had caused her mood, and sensing that she wasn't ready to bare her soul, he started to guess. "Are you upset about Lucy? Her recovery is going slowly and she'll need physical therapy for a long time, but she's doing fine."

"I know."

He played another hunch. "For your information, Abby's contractions stopped. Jennings is keeping her for observation, though."

She nodded. "I checked on her before I left work."

He'd eliminated those two possibilities and with nothing else to go on, he eyed the wine bottle. "You haven't drained the whole thing, have you?"

"One glass is still my limit."

That was a comforting thought. Yet he also knew that Marissa only drank on special occasions. He might not be the most intuitive of men, but this plainly wasn't a night for rejoicing. For whatever reason, she'd broken her rule tonight. With Toby being his usual doggy self and both Lucy and Abby in a stable condition, she didn't have many excuses left.

Other than Pendleton.

Had she learned of his duplicity, just as Kristi had?

He wanted to broach the subject, then decided it would be better if he waited her out. Patience wasn't his strong suit—he wanted to hear the problem so he could fix it and move on.

And if Pendleton was the problem…then he would take matters in his own hands. The man would regret he'd ever thought of playing false with Marissa.

"Have you eaten?" he asked instead.

"Popcorn. Want some?"

From the way a single glass of wine relaxed her, he could only imagine how such a small amount of alcohol would affect her on an empty stomach. "I'd rather have pizza. How about you?"

"I'm not hungry." She leaned her head back and closed her eyes.

"I am." Without giving her an opportunity to gainsay him, he unclipped his cell phone from his belt and phoned in his delivery order. "Twenty minutes," he announced as soon as he'd finished.

"You could have picked it up on your way home," she mentioned.

"I hate to eat alone." She didn't respond. Neither did she seem inclined to chat, so he changed tactics.

"Are you going to tell me what's wrong? Or do I have to drag it out of you?"

"Nothing's wrong."

"I see. You like to sit in the dark."

"It's my house. I can sit in the dark if I want."

"It isn't something you normally do," he reminded her.

"You're not the only one who can turn over a new leaf."

"Ah." He fell silent and spent a few minutes watching a rerun of *The Lucy Show*—Marissa's favorite choice when something weighed heavily on her.

More and more it seemed as if Pendleton was the cause of Marissa's low spirits. If that were the case, then Justin vowed to hang him out to dry.

Marissa stroked Toby's head, grateful for her pet's steady presence. He'd listened to her sad story, commiserated with her and withheld judgment. Dogs truly were a woman's best friend.

Now, if only she could get rid of Justin, she and Toby could be alone. It wouldn't be for some time, though, because he'd ordered a pizza. How like a man to think that food provided the solution to everything.

"Did you stop by for a reason?" she asked. "Because if you didn't, I'm making this an early night."

"I drove by because I was worried when you didn't return my calls. Didn't you get my message?"

She stroked Toby's back. "Sorry. Was it important?"

"I had to cancel our paint date. ER got busy and I filled in."

She'd forgotten all about their project, but she couldn't summon enough energy to apologize. Her whole world had been shaken; she was entitled to forget an appointment or two. "There's always tomorrow night."

"I thought you had plans with Trevor."

This time she didn't bother to correct his use of the wrong name. "Not anymore."

"City business again?"

She managed a laugh. To think she'd been so impressed by Travis's long hours and dedication. Now she could only wonder how many of those late nights he'd actually been working. Somehow everything he'd ever told her seemed suspect, especially when she considered how he hadn't mentioned a word about Tanya until she'd caught them together.

"You could say so," she said.

She would have preferred to share the story after she'd come to terms with the day's events—preferably in the next decade—but with Justin underfoot, she didn't have the option. It was as plain as the dog in her lap that Justin had settled himself in for the duration. Sticking to her silent routine would only delay the inevitable.

"I may as well give you the condensed version," she muttered. "Travis is seeing someone else."

"Oh."

"His secretary."

"I see."

"Actually, she's his administrative assistant."

"Since when?"

"Since before he met me. They'd broken up, but now they're back together."

He scooted closer and hugged her. "I'm so sorry, Mari. I wish I could say something to make you feel better."

"I'm okay. Really." That was debatable, but he didn't need to know it. Suddenly, she realized he hadn't sounded shocked or outraged by her announcement. Her eyes narrowed as she turned to study him. "You don't sound too surprised. Did you know about Travis?"

"I'd heard a rumor," he began.

"When?"

"I went to Kristi's tonight to look for you. She told me about Travis."

Marissa was horrified. "She knows, too?"

"Afraid so."

Inwardly she groaned. "Goody. By tomorrow, I'll be fielding blind dates with Kristi's second cousins twice removed."

"Don't be ridiculous. I'm told the proper mourning period for an unfaithful fellow is three days. Kristi'll wait that long at least."

Marissa managed a smile. "Don't count on it."

"In the meantime, is there anything I can do? Spike his doughnuts with laxative? Squirt super-glue on his executive chair? Smear black shoe polish on his phone?"

The image of Justin sneaking into Travis's office with a stocking cap over his face made her giggle. "Just ruin him, please."

"He's doing that well enough on his own. As soon as people read tomorrow's newspaper, he'll spend his day fielding irate phone calls. He has a lot to answer for and the citizens of Hope are going to hold him accountable."

"Because he cut the mosquito control program?"

"None other," he assured her. "I followed a lead today and passed it on to the reporter. How did you find out?"

"I was in Travis's office when Miller called. I still can't believe Travis was willing to sacrifice people's health for money. When I think of how Lucy and all the rest of our West Nile cases might have not gotten ill if we'd sprayed all over town and not just a few spots, it makes me furious!"

"You aren't the only one," he said darkly. "The man simply has other priorities."

"He needs to get them in order."

"Let's hope so. For what it's worth, Mari, Pendleton wasn't the right man for you."

"Obviously not," she said wryly. "But if you're going to say 'I told you so…'"

"I'm not. But I really thought you'd dump him as soon as you realized that Toby and Travis didn't share a mutual admiration society."

"I should have, but I honestly thought Toby would grow on him."

"Given enough time, maybe, but dogs are a good judge of character. No one can pull the fur over their eyes."

She moved her hand to rub Toby's tummy and he stretched out to allow her greater access. "You're just saying that because Toby likes you," she said.

He grinned. "Of course. Dog-lover or not, look at it this way. Pendleton's girlfriend saved you a lot of grief."

Maybe in the long term, but at the moment the short term was quite painful.

"Do you know the worst part of all this?" she mused. "I feel like such a fool. I saw the same signs you did, but I ignored them."

"Sometimes we see what we want to see."

What a spooky thought. How could she trust her judgment the next time? She clearly had serious flaws when it came to choosing men. "What scares me the most," she said slowly, "is how I'm more like my mother than I'd thought."

"What makes you say that?"

"She always falls in love with the first man who shows an interest in her. No wonder she's been married four times and is working on number five."

"You are not your mom," he said firmly.

She continued as if he hadn't spoken. "I never could understand how she could live her life the way she did but, oddly enough, now I can. The fear of being alone makes a person overlook a lot of faults."

"You aren't alone."

Having his arm around her was as comforting as a warm blanket and a hot fire on a cold night. Yes, she had a lot of good, close friends, Justin included, but she wanted more than a few acquaintances. She wanted a husband, children, a mortgage and a minivan.

She wanted a family.

Unfortunately, once again, the possibility had slipped out of her grasp.

Living with her grandmother and seeing her childhood friends with their parents and siblings had shown her just how much she'd been missing. Well, she was tired of dashing her hopes. If she wasn't destined to have a husband, she could still have the rest of her dream, couldn't she?

Her resolve strengthened. Yes, she could. It would be tough, but she could do it. She *would* do it.

"Well, I won't be alone for too long. I'm going to have a baby," she announced.

Never at a loss for words, Justin couldn't frame a single coherent thought. "You're what?"

Before she could answer, the doorbell shattered the tense moment. "Pizza's here," she said.

A red haze colored Justin's vision as he dealt

with the delivery boy. How could Pendleton have put Mari in such a predicament, then left her? The man was a sorrier excuse for a human than Justin had thought. He deserved something far more than a laxative-laden doughnut. Broken kneecaps, a busted nose and several well-placed punches seemed far more appropriate.

He plunked the flat box onto the coffee table, his appetite gone. "You're pregnant," he said flatly, waiting for—*dreading*—confirmation.

"Not yet."

Once again, he froze, completely confused. "You said you were."

"I said I was going to have a baby. But I'm not pregnant. Not yet."

He held up his hands. "Wait a minute. I'm lost."

"It's quite simple, Justin. I should have thought of this before. I don't have good luck with the men in my life, so I've decided to skip that part of the plan and go straight to having a baby. I'll be thirty soon. My biological clock is ticking."

"Without a male in your equation, how do you expect to become pregnant?"

"I just got the idea, Justin. I haven't worked out

all the details. It shouldn't be too hard to find a donor, though."

She wanted a donor. Heaven help him, but he wanted to be the one she chose. And he wanted to donate the old-fashioned way, not with medical science's syringes and test tubes.

"Did you have someone in mind?" he asked warily, hoping she'd say no and wishing for her to ask him.

She paused. "No. Not really."

The notion of watching her screen prospective men to be the father of her baby was more than he could handle. "I have to tell you, Mari, this is the most ridiculous idea I've ever heard," he said flatly.

"It is not," she defended herself.

"Yes, it is." Unable to contain himself, he clicked off the television with the remote, rose and began to pace. "Just so you'll know, I *wanted* things between you and Pendleton to fall apart."

She sat, stunned. "Why? Didn't you want me to be happy?"

"Of course I did. I was jealous. I didn't want you to be happy with *him*. I wanted you to be happy with *me*."

"But I *am* happy with you, Justin. We would still be friends—"

"Dammit, Mari," he exploded as he ran his hands through his hair. "Don't you get it? I don't want to be a friend. I want to be more." He met her gaze without hesitation.

Her jaw dropped. "More?"

"More," he said firmly. "I've listened to all your reasons why we don't suit, but as far as I'm concerned, every one you listed is wrong. You haven't given us a chance and until you do, I'm not going to stand by and watch you find some other guy to be a sperm donor. If that's what you're thinking, you can put that thought right out of your head!"

Silence reigned for a long minute. Even Toby realized the atmosphere had changed because he now sat up, his ears perked up as if on alert.

"Marissa," he began, but before he could say more than her name, she burst into noisy tears.

Justin winced. This hadn't been the response he'd expected. Surprise, then a gentle smile as her eyes lit up had been the reactions he'd been hoping to see. Then again, his delivery and timing hadn't been the best. He should have wined and dined her first, not blurted his announcement without laying the proper groundwork.

Now she was upset and Justin didn't know why. One thing was for certain: the only thing guaranteed to make a man feel totally at a loss and completely uncomfortable was a woman crying. Neither did it help when Toby stared at him with reproach in his dark doggy eyes. You broke her, now fix her, he seemed to say.

Resigned, Justin crouched beside her. "Aw, honey. You don't have to cry."

"I know." She sniffled, pulling a tissue out of the box to blow her nose. "It's just that I'd waited for years for you to notice me as more than the girl next door."

"Really?" Certain of his success, he grinned.

She nodded as she wiped her eyes. "Yeah."

He stroked the side of her face. "I'm sorry I was such a slow learner."

"Don't worry about it." She brushed at her cheeks and cleared her throat. "In any case, it doesn't matter."

"You're right. We're starting over. This time, we'll—"

She laid a hand on his arm. "That's just it, Justin. There isn't a 'this time.'"

"Wait a minute. What are you saying?"

"We're friends, Justin. As much as I appreciate hearing you say what you did, nothing else would work between us."

CHAPTER EIGHT

"How can you say that?" he demanded.

"Because it's true," Marissa said simply.

"But you said—"

"I know what I said, Justin. And while it's true I'd hoped to be something more than your college friend, those sparks never took hold. Rather than become disappointed and bitter, I accepted things as they were and moved on. You certainly did. Between marriage and med school, you created a life for yourself, too."

"That was then. This is now. And now I can say there are plenty of sparks between us."

Her face warmed as she remembered their kiss. "I'll admit we have a few embers—"

"Embers, hell! We could have started a bonfire!"

"The point is, Justin, good friends don't form

good intimate relationships. Look at Rachel and Ross. They—"

"For God's sake, Mari, Rachel and Ross are television characters. Of course they had issues, problems and rocky spots. Without those, there wouldn't have been a show to watch. Reality is far different than a sitcom."

"And the reality is, how many couples remain on good terms after they've split up?" she asked. He started to speak, but she pressed on. "Are you still good friends with your ex-wife?"

His mouth closed with a decided snap. "I'm right, and you know it," she added.

"What makes you think you'll have a longer-lasting marriage with someone you've just met instead of with someone you've known for years?"

"I don't have any guarantees, but if you and I ever went our separate ways, I would lose a dear friend as well as a husband," she said quietly. "The hole you'd leave in my life is too great to risk. Having your friendship is better than having nothing. I made my decision long ago and I won't change my mind, Justin. I can't."

"You're shortchanging us."

"I don't agree."

"You're settling for second-best."

"I'm playing it safe," she corrected. "The question is, after all this time, why are you suddenly so interested? Travis isn't the first man I've dated in recent years."

"I wasn't ready."

"And you are now."

"Yes."

"Sorry, but I'm not convinced."

"I'm working on my house," he said. "I'm trying to make it a homey place, just like you suggested. You've always accused me of avoiding commitment. This proves I'm not."

"New paint, curtains and a few pieces of furniture don't mean commitment."

"I don't do anything that I don't want to do," he reminded her. "If I wasn't willing, you would have never convinced me to step into a hardware store in the first place."

"And here I thought my powers of persuasion had finally cracked your shell."

"Maybe they did, but, regardless of how it happened, I don't want to go on the way we have been. Our arrangement was fine for a while, but now it's time for a change."

"So you want a change. Why me?" She studied him closely.

"Why not you? We have a lot of history, Mari."

"You've been listening to Lucy, haven't you?"

"No, but the woman is right. We already know each other better than a lot of married people do. Why can't we take the next step? Unless you're running scared," he accused.

"And you're only feeling sorry for me."

"Feeling sorry?" He snorted. "Right now, pity is definitely *not* what I'm feeling. Try exasperated and irritated."

He took several steps closer to loom over her. "Truth is, I'd like nothing more than to carry you off to your bedroom and kiss you senseless. Then I'd love to start going through my list of other things I'd like to do, the first of which is to drive you so wild you can't tell up from down. Pity is the very last thing on my mind!" he ended on a roar.

"Maybe it is, but—"

"Would you stop finding excuses?" he ordered. "Because it's all they are."

"They're not excuses," she insisted.

"Believe me, they are. Arguing won't change that fact."

She jumped to her feet, sending Toby on a defensive scramble to the end of the sofa while she stood toe to toe with him. "Can you hear us? We've only talked about dating for the last few minutes and already you're losing your temper!"

"Because you're too stubborn to see reason."

"And you hate having someone say no to you."

For a long moment, there was silence.

Hating that their conversation had turned into a shouting match, she apologized.

A muscle tensed in his jaw as he nodded, but when he spoke, he'd softened his tone. "I know when I'm right about something and when I'm wrong. I'm right about us."

"Oh, Justin," she began miserably. "I wish I could make you see the situation from my side."

He held up his hands. "I'll admit I had lousy timing to spring this on you tonight after your fiasco with Pendleton, but I never thought you were a quitter, Mari. You're quitting before the game's even begun, and that's not fair to either of us."

It may not be fair, she cried out inside, but it's infinitely safer. She'd taught herself not to imagine him in her mental picture of the future. Letting herself fall back into the old habits she'd conquered was sheer foolishness. Doing so would only make them harder to break the second time.

He took her hands in his. "All I'm asking of you right now is to think about what I said. Mull it over, try it on for size. Then when I ask for a date, you can say yes or no."

She sighed. "Justin, can't you just accept my—"

"No, I can't."

"You're setting us both up for heartache."

"I disagree, but if we can't handle being more than friends, we'll deal with whatever comes next like two mature adults." He hesitated. "Be honest. You'd like to see if we can make this work, too."

She was prepared to deny it. Unfortunately, she couldn't because, heaven help her, she wanted the same thing he did. She must be a complete glutton for punishment.

Surrendering, she opted to set a few terms of her own. "You won't hound me in the meantime?"

"Not one word," he promised. "As long as you keep an open mind. Don't think about what could or couldn't happen. Focus on today."

Could she do it? Would she be able to enjoy the moment and let tomorrow worry about itself? After all, what was the alternative? Having Toby as her sole companion for the next umpteen years? Going on blind dates with Kristi's innumerable relatives and watching Justin fall in love with another woman?

But how could she be sure that he wanted her for herself? That it wasn't because he'd finally realized his lonely state and she was handy?

There was only one way to find out, she supposed. Take each day as it came and wait for a sign. Any sort of sign.

"I'll try," she said.

"And no more talk of finding sperm donors."

"I'm not getting any younger."

"I'm serious, Mari. I don't want you to even *think* about the subject."

"Okay, okay," she grumbled, "but if your idea doesn't work…"

His gaze was intent. "It will, Mari. It will. You can bet the farm on that."

If only she was as certain…

"Am I glad it's Friday," Kristi said fervently as she plonked into a chair and began charting her patient records in the computer. "What a week!"

Marissa looked up from the heart monitor screen of their newest patient. Carter Mosby was thirty-two and had been admitted around three a.m. with all the symptoms of infective endocarditis. His recent dental work had wreaked havoc with his recently repaired heart valve in spite of his prophylactic antibiotic regimen, and now he was very sick.

"I agree," she said.

"Have you finished Dr. St. James's house yet?"

"The furniture is being delivered today," Marissa said. "He wants me to come by and help him arrange it, and then we're officially done."

"Furniture? You must be one persuasive lady."

"Actually, it was his idea." She'd been completely stunned when he'd asked her to help him find the appropriate pieces to fill his living room and bedroom. At first she'd thought he'd use the opportunity to press his suit, but he hadn't acted any differently than normal. They'd fallen back into their easy routine and although she'd spent the evening bracing herself for him to officially ask her for a date, he hadn't.

Here it was, four days later, and he *still* hadn't made any sort of overture. She didn't know if she should be happy or sad.

She should be happy, she decided. She still didn't know if she'd say yes or no and it was easier to let matters slide rather than change the status quo.

At night, though, with only Toby curled up at her feet, she almost wished otherwise.

"What's your next project?" Kristi asked.

"Nothing. It's enough to keep my grass as well as Lucy's under control."

"How's she doing these days?"

"Great. Justin might let her go home tomorrow. She'll need occupational therapy until she's more independent as far as managing at home, but she does fairly well by herself. The hospital social worker has made arrangements for her to have home health nursing visits, along with a host of other services."

"Does she have any family nearby?"

"Her sister is coming to live with her, at least temporarily."

"I'm glad for her. Even with all of her physical limitations, she's still better off than some people." Kristi's gaze shot toward Lonnie Newland's cubicle.

Marissa sighed. "Yes."

"You know," Kristi said softly, "the man is failing before our eyes."

"I know."

"This sounds so cruel and heartless, but I can never understand how we call ourselves humane for not allowing our pets to remain in a similar condition, yet we have a different set of rules for people."

"You'll have to take up the issue with our ethics committee. All I know is that miracles do happen."

Kristi logged off her computer and rose. "If

he's supposed to get one, then I wish it would hurry up and manifest itself. I'm not sure how much more Abby can stand."

Marissa stared through the glass partition. Even from this distance, she could see the tired slump to Abby's shoulders and the circles under her eyes. "I'll try to talk her into resting a bit on the cot down the hall."

"Good luck. I've already offered but she refused."

Marissa went to Lonnie's room. "How are you doing?" she asked Abby.

Abby smiled faintly. "I'm okay. Junior isn't quite as active today."

"Why don't you take thirty minutes and lie down in the other room? The bed isn't the greatest, but at least you'll be able to put your feet up."

"Thanks, but Eric is coming by in an hour to take me home. I don't really want to go…" she stroked her husband's limp hand "…but Eric says that no one can look after the baby except me, and Lonnie's in good hands."

"He's right."

"I just hate to leave him. He's going to be gone

soon and I want to spend every possible minute with him that I can."

Clearly, Abby had come to terms with the terminal state of her husband's condition. "I promise to call you if there's the slightest change," Marissa said kindly.

"His pneumonia is better, isn't it?"

"Yes." She didn't feel compelled to point out that medical science had gained in that area, but had lost ground elsewhere. His seizures had become harder to control.

"People have asked me if I'd known this was going to happen, would I have done anything differently," Abby said.

"And would you?"

"No." She shook her head. "I take that back. Yes, there is one thing. We'd have started our family sooner than we did. We always thought there would be plenty of time. There wasn't."

"We're all guilty of thinking on those lines."

Abby nodded. "My advice to anyone now is to seize the moment. Don't put the important things off. And never let a day go by without telling someone you love them."

A tear rolled down Abby's cheek and she quickly brushed it aside. "Look at me. I'm just a bucket of sunshine today, aren't I? Well, enough of this maudlin stuff."

She pasted on a tired smile. "Did I tell you that Eric helped me finish the baby's room? We're set for the big day."

After listening to Abby talk about the decor of the nursery, Marissa returned to Carter Mosby. "It's time to bother you again," she said cheerfully as she went through her usual routine.

"Has it been an hour?"

"Time flies, doesn't it?" she said, before she listened to his heart. The rumbling murmur she heard fit Justin's diagnosis of mitral valve involvement.

As she replaced her stethoscope around her neck, she smiled at him. "No changes that I can tell. Can I get you anything? More iced water? Another blanket?"

"I'm fine." With that, his head fell to the side as he suddenly went limp and his monitor went flat.

Cardiac arrest!

Instantly Marissa sprang into action. She

slapped the code blue button on the wall, then began CPR. Within seconds, Kristi had wheeled the crash cart into the room and minutes later the small area was filled with staff who'd responded to the overhead announcement.

By the time Justin arrived, Marissa had already put her advanced cardiac life support training to use. She'd defibrillated the patient twice and was already planning her next move.

"What happened?" Justin sounded breathless, as if he'd run the mile in record time.

"We were talking and he just crashed. We're ready to defib for the third time."

One glance at the monitor's unsteady line gave him the condition—ventricular fibrillation. "Go ahead."

She poised the paddles. "Clear!"

No change.

"Let's intubate," he said. As soon as someone placed the endotracheal tube into his hand, he slid it into place.

"Where's the epinephrine?" he asked.

"Going in as we speak," Marissa said, as she pushed the drug into the IV line.

He picked up the paddles. "Here we go. Clear!"

This time, a normal rhythm appeared on the monitor. "I want labs and a blood gas," he ordered one nurse. "And I want someone to call Life Flight. This guy's going on a ride." He turned to another nurse. "See if we have a preliminary report on his blood culture yet. And if we don't, get one!"

Both nurses disappeared while Justin, Kristi and Marissa worked to stabilize the patient. Before long, both women returned.

"Kansas City is ready for him and the helicopter will be taking off shortly," the one reported. "It should be here within twenty minutes."

"Lab says the preliminary culture shows gram positive cocci—probably *Staph aureus*."

"At least we know what we're dealing with," Justin remarked.

"It's treatable, though, isn't it?" Marissa asked. She'd cared for a number of patients with this condition over the years and they'd all recovered.

"Yes, but the bacterial growth has probably formed an embolus which moved to another area of his heart and caused his infarct. He'll need arteriograms and a host of other studies that aren't available here. And if the infection spreads…"

Marissa didn't need the details spelled out. If the infection spread, their patient's prognosis wasn't good.

Fortunately, Carter Mosby remained stable under their watchful eyes, although even if he pulled through without any other complications, he would require IV antibiotics for four to six more weeks.

The cardiac flight team arrived on time and the Hope staff passed on their responsibility with some relief. An hour after Carter's heart attack, he was on his way.

"Anyone for a cup of coffee?" Justin asked.

"I could use one," Marissa said fervently.

"You're in luck." He grabbed her hand and led her into the nursing conference area where a pot of coffee waited.

She sipped the cup he'd poured. "This is awful."

"Yeah, but it's a shot of much-needed caffeine. If it's good stuff you want, I'll take you to the best coffeehouse in town tonight to celebrate my house's new look."

"Is this a date?"

He grinned. "Nope. We may be celebrating, but going out for a cappuccino is not a date."

"I'm not so sure."

"Trust me. It isn't. I'll let you know when it is." He drained his portion and tossed the paper cup into the trash can. "Sorry to run, but I'm already behind. See you at seven?"

"Sure."

"Great." All at once he did something he'd never done before at the hospital. He pressed a hard but quick kiss on her mouth, then disappeared, leaving a stunned Marissa in his wake.

"Are you ready to fly this coop, Miss Lucy?" Justin teased his patient some minutes later.

"I've been ready since the beginning of the week," Lucy said tartly, although the twinkle in her eyes softened the effect.

"Then I'll sign you out first thing in the morning."

"That, my young man, is the best news I've heard all day." She sighed. "I can't wait to see my garden. Smell the roses, let the dirt run through my fingers."

He held up a hand. "Wait a minute. Seeing the

garden and smelling the roses are okay, but letting the dirt run through your fingers has to wait a while. I don't want you tiring yourself out. You're going to have a long recovery as it is. I don't want you to suffer a relapse."

"I won't. My sister is more of a fussbudget than you are," she grumbled.

"She'd better be, or I'll keep you for another week."

"I'll be good. I promise. At least I can sleep in my own bed. I can hardly wait."

He couldn't wait to sleep in his own bed either. Although he wanted Marissa there, too.

"I have to warn you, though. When you see your yard, don't hold us to your gardening standards. We did our best, but we can't compete with a pro like yourself."

"I'm sure you did fine. Beggars can't be choosers, I always say." She leaned forward and lowered her voice. "By the way, how are things going between you two?"

"What makes you think there's anything going on?" he prevaricated.

"She told me about your little heart-to-heart."

"Did she also tell you about her crazy idea to have a baby on her own?"

"Yes."

"I hope you set her straight."

Lucy smiled. "She's afraid of making another mistake. Her mother's antics and poor judgment have made her worry that she's a chip off the old block."

"She's nothing like her mother."

"You and I both know that, but look at it from her side. Every person she's loved has rejected her in one way or another. Her dad died, then her mother dropped her at her grandmother's house like a piece of unwanted luggage, now Travis." She shook her head. "The poor dear. It's hard to jump back in the saddle when you've fallen off so many times."

Inwardly he cringed. He hadn't helped matters either over the years. No wonder she'd given up on him. Well, no more. He wasn't giving up without a fight. "I'm not Pendleton."

"You don't have to convince me," she said.

"That's the problem. I want to show Marissa how much I care about her, but I don't want to go down Pendleton's candy and flowers route. His idea of romance seems too canned and impersonal. Any suggestions?"

"Not at the moment, but Marissa isn't impressed by what money can buy."

"I know. We've always gravitated to the simpler things like renting a movie, going out for ice cream, taking a long walk, but I want to do something different, something unique."

"I understand, but she likes those things, so I'd keep doing them if I were you."

"I still want to give her something more meaningful, more special than a movie rental or a carton of ice cream," he insisted.

"Our time is more valuable than anything we could purchase."

"I'm already spending nearly every waking minute with her." In fact, he wanted the non-waking moments, too. If only he could convince her to agree.

"Hmm. I shall have to think on this. Don't worry. Between the two of us, we'll think of the perfect way to knock her socks off."

Her socks weren't the only thing he wanted

off! Pulling his mind back on track, he said, "Thanks. I owe you one. In the meantime, get a good night's rest so you can go home."

"I will."

He turned to leave, satisfied to have an ally working on his dilemma of finding the perfect gift for Marissa.

"Wait," Lucy called as he reached the doorway. "I have an idea. Two, in fact."

"Fast work. What have you got?"

"How good are you with your hands?"

He grinned. "Depends on what you want me to do with them." He could think of several things, but none of them were appropriate to share. "Brain surgery is out, but everything else I can manage."

"Excellent. There are two things she's wanted for a long time."

Justin listened. The one suggestion wouldn't pose a problem, but the other? It would be tough, but he'd find a way if it was the last thing he ever did.

"Wow, Justin. I'm so impressed with how well this turned out."

Justin couldn't argue. The chocolate brown

leather sofa and matching side chair she'd chosen were made for the room and complemented the wall color and tan-flecked carpeting that she'd also selected. The blue, green and burgundy throw pillows as well as the burgundy drapery scarves gave the room plenty of color. Not a ruffle or a flower in sight.

"It's beautiful and so welcoming. Don't you agree?" she asked.

While the room was awesome in comparison to its previous appearance, he only had eyes for Marissa. "Absolutely."

"Come on. I want another look at your bedroom." She grabbed his hand and led him down the hall to the first door on the right. "Isn't this so much better?" she asked as she twirled around.

He grinned at her delight. "I have to hand it to you, Mari. You did a fantastic job."

"Thanks." She grinned impishly at him. "I never thought your four-poster bed would fit, but it did."

"Where there's a will, there's a way," he said. The truth was, he couldn't have passed up the purchase, no matter what the cost. As soon as he'd seen the bedframe in the store, he'd imagined Mari's lacy unmentionables hanging from the posts as if tossed in reckless abandon.

He was ready for reckless abandon.

Now, watching her smooth the dark green coverlet with gentle, caressing movements was nearly his undoing. Although the air-conditioning had cooled the house, his internal temperature had risen about ten degrees. If he didn't withdraw to a less provocative environment, Marissa would find herself flat on her back, minus her red T-shirt and denim shorts.

And Toby would spend the next several hours in Justin's backyard, barking at birds and chasing squirrels without any human supervision.

"Are you ready to go now?" he asked, his discomfort lending a gruff edge to his voice.

"Yes, but it's a shame we won't stay here and enjoy your new furniture."

God help him, but the desire to make love to her on his leather sofa was becoming downright painful.

"Another night." He ushered her into the hallway, hoping that particular pleasure wouldn't be too long in coming. "I have my mouth set for a French vanilla cappuccino and one of their famous club sandwiches."

"It sounds wonderful" she said. "Do you want to follow me home so I can drop Toby off, or…?"

"Leave him here," he said. "The local cat and squirrel population need the exercise."

"Okay."

Marissa noticed how Justin guided her out to his car, one hand at the small of her back. Funny thing, but he hadn't done that before, had he? No, she decided. If he had, she would have felt those delicious tingles up her spine before now.

Or was she simply seeing him in a new light?

Don't overanalyze this, she cautioned herself. *Enjoy the moment.*

She did.

While parts of their outing took on a more date-like quality, even if Justin denied it, other parts felt familiar. Out of habit, they shared their sandwiches and Justin swapped his dill pickle spear for her serving of potato salad.

"According to the scuttlebutt, Travis Pendleton has taken a lot of heat ever since the article came out in the newspaper," he said as he sipped his cappuccino.

"Really?"

"Yeah. He's not the only one, either. All the city council members have been hearing from their constituents. Unless they change their tunes, I wouldn't be surprised to see all new faces after the next election."

"Rightly so. Maybe they'll think twice before they cut public health programs."

"Something tells me they will." He set his empty cup onto the table. "Shall we go?"

She didn't want to, but they couldn't sit in the coffee shop all night. Neither could they leave Toby outside for hours, causing havoc with the wildlife. "We should," she said, rising. "I'm sure Toby's driven your neighbors crazy with his barking."

He grabbed the ticket, then reached into his back pocket. A sheepish grin appeared on his face. "Um, Mari?"

"Forgot your wallet again?"

He nodded. "You know me too well," he said weakly. "Sorry about that."

She reached into her purse and pulled out several greenbacks. "How can you forget it? What would happen if the cops stopped you and demanded to see your driver's license?"

"The joys of small-town living. They all know who I am. They aren't going to pull me over without a reason and I don't intend to give them one."

"Hmm. Someday, I'm going to forget my purse so you'll be stuck with the bill," she threatened without heat as she slung the strap over her shoulder.

"You won't," he said confidently. "Look at it this way. If this had been a date, you wouldn't have come. Right?"

Her face warmed. "Probably."

"On a *real* date, the man pays for dinner. Because I didn't, that proves this wasn't a date."

She laughed. "If you say so."

Real date or not, she couldn't deny that he'd added a few extra touches, like opening the car door for her and walking with his arm around her waist. She would have commented on those things to prove her point, but she enjoyed them far too much to risk having him stop.

At Justin's house, they found an alert but quiet Toby lying in the grass, vigilantly watching the yard for the first sign of an intruder.

"He's content," Justin remarked.

"Of course. He's in his element, but he's due for a bath."

"There's always tomorrow. I doubt if one more day will make a difference to him."

"Maybe not to him, but if he was sleeping with you, you'd change your tune."

"I stand corrected."

A few minutes later, Marissa stood at the front door with Toby's leash in hand. "I had a nice time, even if I had to pay for it," she teased.

"You're welcome." He grinned. "Annie Tremaine is going to play her bagpipes at the fire station tomorrow night, provided she hasn't been called for an ambulance run. Want to go?"

"Sure, why not?" She hesitated. "Is this a date?"

"Do you want it to be?"

"No," she answered promptly.

"Then it isn't. I'll pick you up at eight-thirty."

She turned to go, wanting a kiss but afraid she'd get one. In the end, she didn't have a choice. He pulled her close and then, without any hesitation or resistance on her part, her lips met his.

The kiss started out slow and gentle, almost as if he was only testing her for a response. Within seconds the featherlight contact had powered up to hard and fast and something that went beyond the boundaries of friendship. All manner of sensations swept over her, as well as an overwhelming urge to feel every inch of him plastered against her body.

Her mind silently begged him to ask her to stay, but her good sense screamed it was too soon. Sleeping with him would only muddy the already murky waters of their quasi-relationship.

Deep down, though, she wanted him inside her as much as she needed air.

Toby's grumble was as effective at interrupting them as a code blue announcement. As they broke apart, Marissa's only consolation came from seeing how Justin's disappointment mirrored her own. "I'll see you tomorrow," she said, making a hasty exit before she did something she'd later regret.

However, if Justin harbored any of those same regrets, he hid them well. Not only did he arrive on time the next evening, but he arrived bearing gifts.

"A chrysanthemum!" she exclaimed. "How did you know I wanted one?"

"You mentioned last week that you had a bare spot in your flower bed. I assumed you and Toby would appreciate it more than cut flowers."

"Really? Why?"

"You'll enjoy planting it and Toby will knock himself out trying to dig it up." He grinned.

While not many men would appear on a girl's doorstep and try to impress her with a potted plant, the chrysanthemum couldn't have been more appropriate. The fact that he'd also chosen one with blooms in her favorite color—yellow—only impressed her more.

"Thank you. This is lovely."

"Glad you like it." He set the pot on the table and dusted off his hands. "We'd better get going or else we won't get within two blocks of the fire station."

As he'd predicted, the crowds had already

gathered around the opened ambulance bay doors. Annie Tremaine, her husband, Jared, and the rest of her crew milled around the growing group of spectators.

Justin spread his blanket under a tree on the edge of the property and sat down with his back resting against the trunk. "Have a seat," he invited, patting the ground beside him.

Marissa sat.

Promptly at nine, as the sun fell behind the treeline, Annie's concert began. Marissa closed her eyes and let the music wash over her, conscious of the man sitting next to her. His clean soap scent mingled with the summer odors of freshly cut grass and burning charcoal briquets. As dusk fell and the temperature dropped several degrees, she instinctively leaned closer to absorb some of his heat.

Before she could object—and she didn't want to—he'd hauled her between his outstretched legs, wrapped his arms around her and held her, spoon fashion.

Perhaps she should have cared about the picture they presented to the world, but she didn't. She was too caught up by his presence, the music and one thought.

If their non-dates all went like this one, she'd be a happy woman.

CHAPTER NINE

On Sunday afternoon, Toby went crazy at the sound of a pickup pulling into the driveway. Marissa didn't recognize the battered vehicle, only the man who'd slid out of the driver's seat wearing a pair of faded blue jeans and a gray T-shirt sporting more holes than Swiss cheese.

"New wheels?" she teased Justin.

"I borrowed Jared and Annie's truck for the day."

"Why?" she asked, curious.

His grin stretched from ear to ear. "Come and see."

She followed him barefoot down the driveway to the rear end and stared with delight at the truckbed's contents. "A tree? Is it for your office?"

"Most certainly not. It's yours."

"Mine?" She couldn't wrap her brain around the idea.

"As gifts go, I'll admit it's unorthodox, but you've been saying how your backyard doesn't have enough shade. I thought this would solve the problem."

"Yes, but—"

"Now you'll have plenty. According to the guy at the greenhouse, this is supposedly the fastest-growing shade tree available. Royal Empress, I believe it's called."

"I've heard of those. When they bloom in the spring, they have lavender flowers, don't they?"

"So I've been told. They're also supposed to grow up to twelve feet during their first season. I figure Toby'll be sitting under shade before the summer's over." He grinned. "Think of all the birds and squirrels he can bark at."

"Now I'll have to invest in a bark collar."

"He's a dog and dogs bark. Plus, it will give him something to lift a leg to. Did you know he squats like a girl dog?"

She ignored his observation. She was still too awed by his gift. "This is so overwhelming. No one's given me a tree before."

"First time for everything," he said cheerfully.

"I don't know what to say."

"Thank you works for me."

"You shouldn't have."

"Why not? You helped with my house. I'm only returning the favor."

"But…"

His satisfied expression changed to one of uncertainty. "You don't like it."

"I do," she insisted. "It's just that—"

"If you don't want the tree, just say so," he interrupted gruffly. "I can handle it."

"I want the tree."

"The nursery will take it back," he continued. "It isn't a problem."

"I want the tree."

"You're certain?" He met her gaze. "You don't have to feel obligated."

"Justin. Read my lips. I want the tree. If I gave you the impression that I didn't, I'm sorry. I'm just so surprised. Of all the things you could have brought me…"

A lump formed in her throat. This was something so unique, so thoughtful, so *Justin*, that her emotions threatened to get the better of her.

He eyed her suspiciously. "You're not going to cry, are you?"

She shook her head, swallowed hard and smiled. "It's perfect. Honest. I couldn't have asked for a nicer surprise." Call her crazy, but fresh flowers and roses were overrated. While they were beautiful and romantic, they simply didn't hold a candle to her Royal Empress tree. The roses would only last for a week, but a tree would serve as a daily reminder of Justin's regard for years. What could be more romantic than that?

"Good." Relief flashed across his face and his satisfied smile returned. In fact, she could almost see his chest swell with pride.

"Do we need to pick out a spot, or did you have one in mind?" he asked.

"I know exactly where it belongs." She slid the shovel off the truckbed while he carried the three-foot tree into the backyard. "Here," she said, thrusting the spade into the ground to mark the spot.

He started to work. Sweat glistened on his arms and face as he created the proper-sized hole for the tree's root ball. The urge to offer her help burned inside her, but his fierce concentration stopped her. He wouldn't appreciate her mother-hen treatment when he was obviously determined to do this by himself, for her.

For *her*.

Only a man who knew her better than she knew herself would have thought of such a gift, or been willing to provide it. If she wasn't careful, she'd fall in love with him all over again.

Oh, who was she trying to kid? She already had.

In fact, she wondered if she'd ever truly stopped, or if she'd only been fooling herself.

The truth flashed in front of her. All his accusations about settling for second-best, being afraid and too stubborn to see reason had described her perfectly. No wonder he'd been so exasperated with her and had refused to listen to her excuses.

Now she could hardly wait for him to ask her on a date. When he did, she intended to say yes without any hesitation or second thoughts.

Certain his invitation wouldn't come until they'd finished their chore, she wanted to hurry the process along.

"You don't need to dig all the way to China," she told him.

"I'm following the instructions. I have to break up the soil so air and the fertilizer can get to the roots," he huffed as he dumped another spadeful of dirt on top of the growing pile.

Toby barked as he danced around them, clearly excited by this new activity.

"Is this where I make jokes about you becoming a tree surgeon?" she teased.

"Very funny."

Conscious of his weaker arm, she tried to spell him. "I'll take a turn."

"No, you won't. I'm almost done."

"This can't be the physical therapy your doctor had in mind," she pointed out.

"Maybe not, but it's just as effective. If you want to do something useful, you can keep Toby out from underfoot."

The terrier was either growling at the shovel and trying to bite it, or pawing at the fresh earth as if attempting to help. Either way, he was being a royal nuisance.

Marissa picked up her dog. "Come on, Tobe. Let's make a pitcher of lemonade."

By the time she returned, Justin had lowered

the tree into the hole and was starting to pack the dirt around its roots. For the next several minutes they worked in silence until the tree stood firmly in its new home. After soaking the ground with the garden hose, he pronounced his job done.

Because it was a warm, humid day, he drained his glass of lemonade in one fell swoop. As she poured another, she waited impatiently for his next invitation.

Instead, he wiped away the beads of sweat on his face and said, "It really is hot."

Perhaps if she coaxed him a bit… "Stay for dinner?"

He crinkled his face apologetically. "I can't. I'm going back to Jared's to help him with a few things. I'll take a rain check, though."

She couldn't deny her disappointment, but chose to hide it. "Okay."

Although he hadn't said he'd drop back by, she'd fully expected him to do so. Unfortunately, he didn't. Yet, as she prepared for bed that evening, she consoled herself with the prospect of seeing him the next day.

On Monday, she greeted him on his rounds

Marissa wanted to do. Yet, realistically, Abby was only prolonging the pain because whether she wanted to admit it or not, she'd lost the essence of what had made Lonnie her husband months ago. Only his body had refused to leave at the same time.

"I'll talk to her," Marissa agreed.

As soon as the handover was complete, Marissa reluctantly entered Lonnie's cubicle. To her experienced eye, his body seemed more frail than usual, as did Abby's.

"Aren't you here a little early?" Marissa asked. "It's only five a.m."

"Early, late." Abby waved her hand carelessly. "Time doesn't mean anything anymore. It all runs together."

Marissa busied herself with her patient's monitors, noticing that his bottom lip was cracked and bleeding from the pressure of his endotracheal tube. She took time to smear ointment on it.

"I understand that Dr. St. James told you Lonnie's prognosis."

Abby grimaced. "He suggested removing his life support."

with a huge smile, and the rest of her shift passed on an upbeat note. When he stopped by that evening to check on Lucy, she waited for him to suggest an outing.

He left without inviting her for so much as an ice-cream cone.

Tuesday would be the day, she thought. However, it, too, came and went without mention of any evening activity whatsoever. Although to be fair, she only saw him for the ten minutes it took to make his rounds through the ICU.

"Continue my orders on Lonnie," he told her. "And call me if anything changes."

Before she could say, "Yes, Doctor," he was gone.

By Wednesday, she was becoming impatient. She invited him to join her as she took Toby to the park, but he declined without giving a reason.

How could she ever accept a date if he never offered?

And because he never offered, her insecurities sprouted like the weeds in Lucy's garden. Had he changed his mind? Decided that he didn't want to change the status quo? Or had they drifted so far into their easy relationship that he was taking her for granted? That a courtship really didn't matter because she was like money in the bank?

Stop worrying, she told herself. He was simply having a busy week, and she was fretting over nothing.

She also had the added problem of Kristi, who'd noticed how she jumped whenever the phone rang and watched the clock when he was due to make rounds.

She'd become truly pathetic.

"You have to shake yourself out of your blue funk," Kristi told her on Wednesday afternoon. "Travis Pendleton isn't worth one minute of regret. You're better off without him."

"You're right," Marissa agreed, not bothering to correct Kristi's mistaken impression. Her situation with Justin was still too new and too tenuous for her to share with anyone, even her closest friend.

At that moment she vowed to stop stewing over the situation. It was counterproductive. Besides, worry never changed anything.

On Thursday, her personal life took a backsea to the crisis with the Newlands…

"He's having seizures every ten minutes now," the night nurse explained during the shift report. "If he lasts twenty-four hours, I'll be surprised."

"Have you called Dr. St. James?" Marissa asked.

"At midnight. He visited with Mrs. Newland, but I don't think he got anywhere."

Marissa didn't need her colleague's comment explained. Justin had been trying to prepare Abby for the inevitable ever since Lonnie's seizure activity had increased in spite of the anti-convulsant cocktails he'd been receiving. In the last couple of days he'd developed a urinary tract infection and his pneumonia had returned with a vengeance. His entire body had become a breeding ground for bacteria and this time medicine wasn't winning the battle.

It was time to let him go.

"You two are friends," the night nurse continued. "Maybe you can convince her."

Yeah, right. As if convincing a woman to give up the love of her life was something

Marissa knew there were times to listen and times to speak. This seemed to be a time to listen.

Abby sighed as she held Lonnie's hand. "Eric thinks I should follow Dr. St. James's advice."

"What do you want to do?" Marissa asked.

She didn't answer at first. "We both have living wills, you know."

Marissa did. Out of the corner of her eye, she saw Justin silently slip into the cubicle. Although he looked as if he'd just showered and shaved, his small smile didn't dispel the weariness in his eyes.

"When he first had the accident," Abby said quietly, "the doctors gave us hope. I was pregnant, so I insisted on doing everything possible for him." She hesitated. "Then things changed. I was the only one who still believed he would improve enough for us to have a life together."

She pressed on her stomach and inhaled deeply. "If we take him off the ventilator, how long will he have?"

Justin answered. "It's hard to say. It might be minutes. It might be hours. Truly though, considering what's going on inside his brain, I don't think a ventilator will make much of a difference."

Suddenly Abby doubled over, clutching her abdomen. Marissa exchanged a glance with Justin before she placed her hands on Abby's shoulders. "The baby's coming, isn't it?"

Abby finally straightened, then nodded. "I've had contractions since ten o'clock last night. I was hoping they'd stop, but…"

"You should be home in bed."

She shook her head. "I had to be here with Lonnie. Even if he hadn't taken a turn for the worse, this seemed the best place to be. If the contractions didn't stop, I wouldn't have far to go to have the baby."

"How far apart are they?" Justin asked.

"Not long. Five minutes."

Five minutes. If they didn't do something soon, she might be helping Justin deliver a baby.

"You're going to OB," Marissa said firmly. "Now."

"Okay." A sheen of perspiration dotted Abby's brow. "But you both have to promise me something first."

Marissa already suspected the request. "If it's possible."

"Don't let him go until after I get back."

Once again, Marissa exchanged glances with Justin. They couldn't predict how long Lonnie would stay with them and it was questionable if Abby's own obstetrician would agree to her running around the hospital so soon after giving birth. Provided she had an uncomplicated delivery in the first place.

"That may not be possible," he began.

Abby gripped Marissa's hand so tightly that her bones ached. "Promise."

"We promise," Marissa said, silently challenging Justin to contradict her.

"We'll do our best," he said, although clearly he had serious doubts about his ability to honor her request.

"I have another favor to ask." Another contraction gripped Abby and she panted until it passed. "Stay with him, please? I don't want him to be alone if, if…if he goes before I get back. I'm not complaining about the other nurses, but I can tell how they've distanced themselves from him. You're the only one who hasn't."

Marissa knew it was a common phenomenon.

Nurses were people, too, and some patients pulled at their heartstrings more than others. Distancing oneself was a coping mechanism so they could do their job without falling apart.

"I won't be more than a few steps away," Marissa promised.

"Thank you."

As soon as Abby released Marissa's hand, Marissa squeezed her shoulders. "I'll get a wheelchair so you can go and have that baby!"

A few minutes after Marissa had called, a nurse from Labor and Delivery had come to wheel Abby to her ward. Eric had been summoned as well, and was on his way to act as Abby's labor coach.

"Do you think Lonnie will hang on long enough for Abby to deliver?" she asked Justin in the nurses' station.

"For Abby's sake, let's hope so."

"What if we increase his seizure meds?"

"He's already at the maximum dosage. If I give him any more, he'll become toxic and we'll do more harm than good. The idea is to help him hang on, not hurry the end along."

"Then what can we do?"

"Nothing, except wait and hope Abby's labor doesn't take hours. He doesn't have many left."

Marissa glanced in Lonnie's direction. "Then it'll happen today."

"His heart rate is already slowing." He traced the blip on the nurses' screen. "It's only a matter of time."

Deep down, Justin's prediction resonated in her heart. "It's strange how fate brings one person into the world while it takes another."

"'To everything there is a season,'" he quoted.

"Yeah, it's just a shame that both seasons have to happen on the same day in the same family."

"One of the great mysteries of life." He passed the latest lab report to her. "You know how to reach me."

She took the piece of paper, then gasped as she saw the cuts and scrapes on his hands. "Justin!" she exclaimed. "What have you done to yourself?"

He stretched out his fingers as if seeing them for the first time. "Oh, this? It's nothing."

"Nothing?" she all but screeched.

He immediately thrust his hands in his pockets. "I've been working in my garage," he said.

Something in his statement didn't ring true. She couldn't imagine what he might be doing that would cause his hands to become so battered. "You haven't taken up boxing, have you?"

He stared at her as if she'd sprouted an extra eye. "Boxing? I don't think so."

"Then what—?"

"If you must know, I've been clumsy," he said, plainly irritated by his admission. "Can we stop the inquisition now?"

"If you insist. I hope you disinfected those cuts."

"I'm a doctor, remember?"

"And I'm a nurse. I know doctors are horrible patients from firsthand experience."

"Well, I'm fine. If you want to worry about someone, worry about Abby. Call if you need me."

As it happened, Justin phoned her throughout the day for updates, instead of waiting for her to call him.

"No baby yet," she informed him at noon after she'd given her hourly report to Eric, who in turn passed it along to Abby. "Lonnie's heart rate has dropped again, so I hope Abby's baby hurries."

At five p.m., just as Marissa was about to go off

duty, Eric phoned. "Abby had a little boy," he said, sounding tired yet happy. "He's on the scrawny side at five and a half pounds, but he'll grow."

"Healthy?" she asked.

"His Apgar scores were eight, then ten," he reported, "whatever that means. I guess it's good."

It was. Ten was the optimal number and indicated that the baby's heart rate, breathing, color, response to stimuli and muscle tone were normal.

"And Abby?"

"She's tired, but okay. She wants to come back to ICU right away, but her doctor says she has to wait a few hours. How's Lonnie?"

"Holding on," she said simply. Which was all she could say. Lonnie's seizures had continued and she'd spent most of her time tending to the necessities of keeping his airway open and his flailing extremities from harm. His heart rate had dropped into the twenties, but how fast it would continue its descent was anyone's guess.

"I don't know how much resting Abby will manage, but call if you think he's only got minutes. Abby will be there, no matter what her doctor says."

Marissa crossed her fingers, hoping it wouldn't come to that.

She handed over her responsibilities to the next shift's nursing staff, clocked herself out, then returned to Lonnie's bedside where Justin found her at six.

"You're still here," he said.

"I couldn't leave. I promised Abby."

"When will Jennings let her visit?"

Marissa glanced at the clock. "An hour, give or take."

"Hungry?" he asked. "I can grab something from the cafeteria."

"I'll pass. I don't feel like eating."

He snaked his arm around her waist. "How are you holding up?"

"I'm all right." For the most part, she performed her duties by rote and with objectivity. However, if she put herself in a situation like Abby's, imagining Justin wasting away like a living corpse, the tears flowed.

"How about some coffee?" As she shook her head, he pushed her toward the door. "Take a break. You need one."

"I can't leave."

"Yes, you can. I'll stay with him. You haven't stepped foot outside all day and a bit of fresh air will do you good. Doctor's orders."

Maybe the feel of the sun against her face would banish the coldness that had settled in her heart. "Okay, but I'm only taking five minutes."

In the end, she was gone for ten. She'd hardly returned when Eric wheeled Abby and her baby into the cubicle. For a few minutes, the excitement of the new life in the new mother's arms overshadowed all else.

"Isn't he handsome?" Marissa exclaimed at the baby's wrinkled face as he slept.

"He is." Abby smiled down at him as she stroked his downy cheek. "His name is Nathaniel. Nathaniel Alonzo Newland. Lonnie was short for Alonzo."

"What a wonderful legacy. He would be pleased."

"I think so, too."

Marissa and Justin moved to the end of the bed to allow Abby access to her husband. Eric wheeled her closer and helped her place young

Nathaniel on the bed next to his father. This would be the closest he would ever be to the man who'd given him life.

"Here's your son, Lonnie," Abby told her husband softly. "He looks just like you."

So touched by the scene, Marissa struggled to swallow the emotional knot in her throat before she slipped out of the room.

As if Justin had sensed her tenuous hold on her control, he followed her into the empty nurses' station and tugged her against him. For a few long seconds, she drew comfort from his presence.

"I'm okay," she finally said. "For a minute, it got to me."

"Yeah, I know."

"It felt like we were intruding to watch Abby introduce her son to her husband. I couldn't stay."

"I understand."

Marissa glanced back at the small family and watched them through the glass. "I'm surprised Lonnie hasn't had another seizure by now."

"I am, too. But look at his heart rate."

The white line showed only an occasional blip.

Eric appeared at the counter, strain evident on his face. "Abby wants you."

Inside the cubicle, Abby had one question. "Can you take out his breathing tube?" she asked.

At this stage, the tube's presence wouldn't matter in the final outcome.

"If you'll step outside, Marissa and I will remove it," Justin said. "It will only take a few minutes."

By the time they'd finished unhooking Lonnie from everything except an IV and his status monitors and had returned to the nurses' station, a staff nurse from the newborn nursery arrived with a bassinet for the baby.

"If he starts to fuss, call us and we'll take him back," she told Marissa. "I'm not sure how healthy it is for him to be up here, exposed to all the germs, but under the circumstances, how could we say no?"

The hours dragged by. Marissa kept her vigil outside the cubicle. Although she was officially off duty, she performed Lonnie's nursing duties anyway. Having another person, a relative stranger to Abby, in the middle of the situation didn't seem right.

"You can go home," she told Justin. "All that's left is the waiting."

"If you're staying, I will, too," he insisted. "I can watch television here as easily as I can at home."

At eight o'clock, Nathaniel needed a bottle and a diaper change, which the nursery staff happily provided. As soon as he was comfortable, he fell asleep in his bassinet once again, completely unaware of the drama taking place.

By eleven-thirty, Lonnie's heart rate had slowed to ten. Determined to give Abby privacy for these final moments, Marissa drew the curtains and left the room.

The two nurses on duty quietly went about their business, leaving Justin and Marissa alone for the most part. The monitor provided the only information about what was going on in Lonnie's cubicle. Marissa watched the number on the screen drop to five and in the next heartbeat the line went flat.

Marissa glanced at the clock. "Three minutes to midnight. What a shame he couldn't have lasted a bit longer. Nathaniel shouldn't celebrate his birthday on the same day his father died."

"He won't." Justin glanced at his wrist.

"According to my watch, it's twelve-oh-two. Tomorrow."

She eyed the wall clock. Its hands had not reached the midnight hour. "You can't falsify a death certificate."

"Who said we're falsifying anything? We found him at twelve-oh-two. No one will quibble over a few minutes."

His thoughtfulness brought tears to her eyes. He was definitely a man worth loving.

"Thank you," she said. "For them."

At twelve-oh-two, Justin walked into the cubicle to do his duty. At twelve-oh-seven, young master Nathaniel wailed and demanded attention, which he promptly received.

Ready or not, life went on.

"You're terribly quiet today," Lucy remarked several days later.

Marissa turned away from the window overlooking Lucy's garden. "I am? I don't mean to be."

"I'm sure it's hard to lose a patient."

She stared at Lucy, incredulous. "How did you know?"

"I read the newspaper. From what I could tell, though, as sad as it is, I'd say the poor man's passing was a blessing."

"It was."

"So why the long face?"

She couldn't keep her frustration from bubbling over. "Justin is driving me crazy! He tells me that I can't see any other man but him, yet I've hardly seen him all week!"

Lucy's grin stretched across her wrinkled face. "I'm sure he has a good reason for his absence."

"If he does, he's not sharing it with me," she grumbled.

"And that bothers you."

"Of course it does! I love the man and he hasn't even asked me out on an official date!"

"Why do you suppose he hasn't?"

Marissa threw up her hands and began to pace the small kitchen. "Who knows?"

"Tell me this." Lucy folded her hands in her lap. "When he told you that he wanted you all to himself, didn't you have doubts?"

"Yes, but—"

"And if he'd asked you out on one of your so-called *official* dates, what would you have said?"

"No," she reluctantly admitted.

"There's your answer. He isn't any more fond of rejection than you are. He's probably waiting until he's sure you won't refuse."

"I won't."

"You and I both know that, but *he* doesn't."

"He would if he'd stick around long enough to find out. Maybe he's not interested anymore. Changed his mind…"

Lucy clicked her tongue, as if instructing a slow student. "I'm going to spell this out because you're missing my point. You're a take-charge sort, otherwise you wouldn't be where you are today. Am I right?"

Marissa thought for a second. "I suppose so."

"In other words, you've gone after what you wanted."

"Yes," she said slowly, trying to follow Lucy's train of thought.

"Now, compare that woman to the one who sat back in college and waited for Justin to notice her. The same woman is still waiting for him to make the next move when it's her turn."

"Ah." Understanding dawned. "I see your point."

"Exactly. You normally take the initiative when it comes to other parts of your life, yet when he's involved, you don't. Why not?"

Lucy was right. "I don't know," Marissa admitted sheepishly. "I guess I thought it was his place."

"Maybe in my century but not in yours," Lucy said firmly. "Young women have more gumption, more interest in controlling their destinies. You, my dear, have a choice. You can either keep waiting like you have been and waste more time, or you can go after the prize."

Lucy's eyes twinkled. "Frankly, if I had a prize like Justin in my sights, I wouldn't be dilly-dallying on a beautiful Sunday afternoon with an old woman."

Seize the moment. Hadn't that been Abby's advice? Hadn't Marissa learned anything from the Newlands?

"I'll do it." Her heart skipped an excited beat. "Will you watch Toby for me? And if I'm not back by dinnertime, can you give him his food? The bag is—"

Lucy brushed aside her instructions. "I know where his food is. Don't worry about Toby, and, by all means, don't hurry back. I wouldn't mind having a personal heating pad to warm my toes tonight if you two care to warm a few things of your own."

Marissa's face reddened. "Lucy!"

"I'm serious. Harriet and I will take good care of your dog. I'll expect you, on the other hand, to take good care of Justin." She motioned to the door. "Now, run along. I'd like to have a few minutes of peace and quiet before Harriet gets back and talks my ear off."

Marissa giggled. "I will."

"Don't forget to spritz on your delicious perfume before you go."

"I won't."

"And, Marissa?" As she paused at the threshold, Lucy added, "For your information, a man who plants a tree intends to be around long enough to watch it grow."

CHAPTER TEN

MARISSA did more than spritz on her favorite perfume. She changed into her above-the-knee, slim-fitting khaki skirt and a sleeveless yellow blouse, replaced her flip-flops with leather sandals, brushed her hair until it hung perfectly on her shoulders and clipped a pearl necklace around her throat.

She felt as nervous as she had when she'd sat for her state nursing boards. Her personal future was as uncertain now as her professional future had been then. In both situations, failure spelled disaster. And also in both, failure simply wasn't an acceptable option.

Justin didn't answer her knock, but she heard a rhythmic pounding coming from the garage. The side door stood open, so she meandered toward it in the hope of finding him.

He was there, his back to her as he stood over something, with a hammer in his hand and muttering about crooked nails. Sawdust covered the cement floor and the scent of freshly cut lumber hung in the air. He positioned another nail with his left hand—his weaker hand—and she heard it land on the floor with a metallic ping. Another round of muttered curses followed as he selected another nail from the small paper bag resting on a nearby overturned bucket.

His poor, battered hands now made sense.

"Hi," she said from the doorway.

He swivelled toward her, eyes wide with surprise. "Marissa. What are you doing here?"

"I haven't seen you for a while and thought I'd drop by." She walked across the double-car garage. "What are you doing?"

He laid the hammer on the workbench and moved just enough to block her view. "Working on a project with Jared."

"May I see?"

"It isn't finished."

"I don't mind."

"It's for you." He sounded both nervous and proud.

"For me? Then I have to see it, finished or not." She sidestepped him and found a four-foot garden planter designed as a mini wishing well. It was exactly what she'd dreamed of setting in her backyard flower bed.

Realizing what he'd done, what he'd put himself through for her, took her breath away. "Oh, Justin."

"Do you like it? Jared helped me cut boards and so forth, but it's my first project and it's not quite square for some reason."

"It's beautiful."

"There are a few crooked nails, well, more than a few, and a couple of—"

Marissa flung one arm around his neck and touched his mouth with her fingers. "It's beautiful. Perfect. And I won't allow you to say otherwise."

He grinned. "Okay. Then you really like it?"

"Absolutely. How did you know I wanted one?"

"Lucy gave me the idea."

She laughed. "Lucy has given you a lot of ideas lately, hasn't she?"

"They've all been good."

She couldn't argue with that. "I'm completely awed by what you've done."

"It's only a planter, not the Taj Mahal."

"I don't care. You've worked on something so difficult and so physically challenging just for me. You could have done something horrible to yourself in the process, like sawn off a finger or crushed a bone or—"

"I may not have my former grip, but I'm not completely inept," he chided.

"But power tools? You could have drilled a hole in your hand and then where would your medical career be?"

He rested his hands on her hips and pulled her close. "I didn't, and my career is just fine. You worry too much."

"Probably," she admitted.

"Just to reassure you, I won't be taking up carpentry as a regular hobby. In future, I'm going to leave woodworking to the experts."

"Do that." A thought occurred to her. "This is why I haven't seen you all week, isn't it?"

"Yeah. It's taken longer to finish than I thought

it would. My patients kept me busier than usual, too, so I didn't get out here as often as I'd planned."

Her doubts vanished and she felt foolish for entertaining them in the first place.

His hands tightened around her. "You imagined all the wrong sort of things, didn't you?"

She hated to admit it aloud. "I'd thought you'd changed your mind about us."

"I hadn't." He eyed her carefully. "If that was running through your mind, why did you come today? To catch me with another woman?"

"No!" Horrified by his accusation, she broke out of his embrace. "Not that. Not that at all."

"Then why?"

Her opportunity was knocking. She drew a deep breath and squared her shoulders. "When you brought the tree, I realized something. I had never gone on a date with the man I love. I waited all week for you to ask me, but you were busy and we hardly saw each other."

"I'm sorry, Mari. If I'd known…"

"It's okay. Anyway, Abby once told me to seize the moment. So, rather than wait for you to make the first move, I chose to make it instead, which is why I came."

She paused. His expression was inscrutable, but she'd waded too far into this particular pool to quit now.

"Justin," she began formally, "would you care to join me for dinner at D'Angelo's tonight?"

"You love me?"

"Yes," she said honestly.

"You're one hundred percent certain?"

Apparently she wasn't the only one who'd suffered doubts. "One hundred percent," she repeated. "But I didn't say it to coerce you or make you feel obligated—"

"I don't," he interrupted. "The only pressure I felt was when I thought time was running out. I've never been so nervous in all my life as when I thought you and Pendleton would tie the knot."

"You were?"

"Sure. I couldn't imagine a life without you."

"Oh, Justin," she murmured. "I can't, either. But before we get too carried away, I need you to be sure of something. If you only want us to be together because we've drifted into a comfortable routine and I'm convenient, then you're doing this for the wrong reasons. We both deserve more than that."

"I haven't drifted into anything. I love you, Mari. I never thought I'd say those words again, much less mean them, but I do."

"Oh, Justin." She sniffled, hardly able to believe she was hearing those words from a man who'd once thought that love didn't exist.

"You aren't going to cry, are you?"

She shook her head and brushed the tears of joy out of her eyes.

"As for a comfortable routine or you being convenient," he continued, "those words don't describe the way I think of you. 'Exciting' and 'sexy' spring to mind."

"Sexy?" Her face warmed. "Really?"

"Yeah. Imagine a seduction so breathtaking and physically exhausting that you'll need a week to recover, and you'll know what I'm talking about."

The garage echoed with his sincerity.

Once again, she found herself plastered to his chest, her head nestled under his chin. She couldn't imagine a better place to be. "Oh, Justin. We've both been so blind and foolish."

"And stubborn."

"And stubborn," she agreed.

"We've corrected our mistakes. That's all that matters."

She raised her head. "Actually, we still have an unresolved issue. Are we going on a date tonight or not?"

"Well, now," he drawled. "I'm all for your idea about D'Angelo's, as long as you're willing to go along with mine afterward."

"Which is?"

"How does a seduction sound?"

A tingle skittered down her spine and her pulse pounded hard in her throat. "It sounds perfect. On second thought, I vote we skip my suggestion and go straight to yours."

"A woman after my own heart." He pressed fervent kisses along her neck. "Your place or mine?"

Her knees would have given out if he hadn't been holding her. "I've always wanted to sleep in a four-poster bed."

"I hate to disappoint you, but we won't be sleeping." He swung her up in his arms. "At least, not for a very long time."

"Promises, promises," she teased.

He stopped at the door. "Toby. What have you done with him?"

"He's having a sleepover at Lucy's. At her request, I might add."

He chuckled. "I should have known."

"Know this," she grumbled at the delay. "You're taking entirely too long and talking far too much."

"Yes, ma'am."

Her second thoughts ceased to exist. This was what she wanted. This was what she'd dreamed of. This was what felt more right than anything she'd ever done.

Before she knew it, he was lowering her down his body ever so slowly, as if he wanted to raise her anticipation to fever pitch.

His plan worked because clothes instantly flew in every direction. Arms and legs tangled as they tumbled onto the comforter-covered mattress. His mouth worked magic, first on her mouth, then as it trailed down her neck to her breasts, teasing, tasting, and tormenting her until she thought she'd go crazy.

His hands—what gifted hands!—stroked and caressed until her skin felt on fire.

But the experience wasn't one-sided. Her mouth was as eager as his; her hands were equally busy exploring the planes of his hard body.

Her curves fit his hollows like interlocking puzzle pieces as she accepted him. Intense pleasure swept her to heights she'd never reached, until she thought she'd shatter into a thousand pieces. This was more than a few sparks. This was an all-consuming fire.

Later—she couldn't say how much later—the blaze died down and left her feeling both replete and exhausted, just as he'd promised. The empty spot in her heart had been filled to overflowing.

"What's the sigh for?" he asked, as he pulled the sheet over them.

"Relief. I'd have missed out on all this if I'd ignored Abby's advice and played it safe."

"Maybe not. I'd have worn you down eventually."

"You sound sure of yourself."

"Of course. I almost let you slip through my fingers. I wasn't going to risk it again. I would have volunteered to be a sperm donor if you'd asked."

"No kidding?"

"Yeah, but only as a last resort. I wanted my ring on your finger first."

"Staking your territory?" she teased.

"Making you mine," he corrected. "I love you, Mari, which is why we're going to have the shortest engagement in history."

Arguing seemed pointless. Even if she'd wanted to, she was too relaxed to care. "How long?"

"A week."

"We won't be able to have a honeymoon," she warned. "I have to give a month's notice if I want time off."

"Then we'll go when we can. We've waited too long to be together as it is."

He was right. They had nothing to gain by postponing the start of their life together and everything to lose. Lonnie's legacy to them was a simple, timeless truth.

Life was too short to waste a single moment.

MEDICAL™

─╴╱╲╴─ *Large Print* ─╴╱╲╴─

Titles for the next six months…

May

THE MAGIC OF CHRISTMAS	Sarah Morgan
THEIR LOST-AND-FOUND FAMILY	Marion Lennox
CHRISTMAS BRIDE-TO-BE	Alison Roberts
HIS CHRISTMAS PROPOSAL	Lucy Clark
BABY: FOUND AT CHRISTMAS	Laura Iding
THE DOCTOR'S PREGNANCY BOMBSHELL	Janice Lynn

June

CHRISTMAS EVE BABY	Caroline Anderson
LONG-LOST SON: BRAND-NEW FAMILY	Lilian Darcy
THEIR LITTLE CHRISTMAS MIRACLE	Jennifer Taylor
TWINS FOR A CHRISTMAS BRIDE	Josie Metcalfe
THE DOCTOR'S VERY SPECIAL CHRISTMAS	Kate Hardy
A PREGNANT NURSE'S CHRISTMAS WISH	Meredith Webber

July

THE ITALIAN'S NEW-YEAR MARRIAGE WISH	Sarah Morgan
THE DOCTOR'S LONGED-FOR FAMILY	Joanna Neil
THEIR SPECIAL-CARE BABY	Fiona McArthur
THEIR MIRACLE CHILD	Gill Sanderson
SINGLE DAD, NURSE BRIDE	Lynne Marshall
A FAMILY FOR THE CHILDREN'S DOCTOR	Dianne Drake

◉™ MILLS & BOON®
Pure reading pleasure

0408 LP 2P P1 Medical

MEDICAL™

—∿— *Large Print* —∿—

August

THE DOCTOR'S BRIDE BY SUNRISE   Josie Metcalfe
FOUND: A FATHER FOR HER CHILD   Amy Andrews
A SINGLE DAD AT HEATHERMERE   Abigail Gordon
HER VERY SPECIAL BABY   Lucy Clark
THE HEART SURGEON'S SECRET SON   Janice Lynn
THE SHEIKH SURGEON'S PROPOSAL   Olivia Gates

September

THE SURGEON'S FATHERHOOD SURPRISE   Jennifer Taylor
THE ITALIAN SURGEON CLAIMS HIS   Alison Roberts
BRIDE
DESERT DOCTOR, SECRET SHEIKH   Meredith Webber
A WEDDING IN WARRAGURRA   Fiona Lowe
THE FIREFIGHTER AND THE SINGLE MUM   Laura Iding
THE NURSE'S LITTLE MIRACLE   Molly Evans

October

THE DOCTOR'S ROYAL LOVE-CHILD   Kate Hardy
HIS ISLAND BRIDE   Marion Lennox
A CONSULTANT BEYOND COMPARE   Joanna Neil
THE SURGEON BOSS'S BRIDE   Melanie Milburne
A WIFE WORTH WAITING FOR   Maggie Kingsley
DESERT PRINCE, EXPECTANT MOTHER   Olivia Gates

 MILLS & BOON®
Pure reading pleasure

0408 LP 2P P2 Medical